SCANDALS,
RUMORS, LIES

Other books in the
CANTERWOOD CREST SERIES:

TAKE THE REINS

CHASING BLUE

BEHIND THE BIT

TRIPLE FAULT

BEST ENEMIES

LITTLE WHITE LIES

RIVAL REVENGE

HOME SWEET DRAMA

CITY SECRETS

ELITE AMBITION

CANTERWOOD
CREST

SCANDALS, RUMORS, LIES

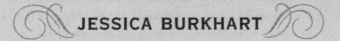 JESSICA BURKHART

ALADDIN M!X
New York London Toronto Sydney

This book is a work of fiction. Any references to historical events, real people, or real locales are used fictitiously. Other names, characters, places, and incidents are the product of the author's imagination, and any resemblance to actual events or locales or persons, living or dead, is entirely coincidental.

m!x

ALADDIN M!X

Simon & Schuster Children's Publishing Division

1230 Avenue of the Americas, New York, NY 10020

First Aladdin M!X edition November 2010

Copyright © 2010 by Jessica Burkhart

All rights reserved, including the right of reproduction

in whole or in part in any form.

ALADDIN is a trademark of Simon & Schuster, Inc., and related logo

is a registered trademark of Simon & Schuster, Inc.

ALADDIN M!X and related logo are registered trademarks

of Simon & Schuster, Inc.

For information about special discounts for bulk purchases, please

contact Simon & Schuster Special Sales at 1-866-506-1949

or business@simonandschuster.com.

The Simon & Schuster Speakers Bureau can bring authors to your live event.

For more information or to book an event contact the Simon & Schuster Speakers

Bureau at 1-866-248-3049 or visit our website at www.simonspeakers.com.

Designed by Jessica Handelman

The text of this book was set in Venetian 301 BT.

Manufactured in the United States of America 0111 OFF

2 4 6 8 10 9 7 5 3

Library of Congress Control Number 2010911662

ISBN 978-1-4424-0384-0

ISBN 978-1-4424-0385-7 (eBook)

To Team Canterwood for supporting the series! Best. Readers. Ever.

xoxo

ACKNOWLEDGMENTS

Thank you to everyone at Simon & Schuster, including Bethany Buck, Fiona Simpson (my fave Gleek), Liesa Abrams, Venessa Williams (*bows to Venessa's marketing genius*), Mara Anastas, Lucille Rettino, Bess Braswell (miss you!), Katherine Devendorf, Ellen Chan, Alyson Heller, Jessica Handelman, Karin Paprocki, Russell Gordon, Dayna Evans, and my fabulous copyeditor, Valerie Shea, who is both fabulous and ever-ready ☺.

Kate Angelella, I'd never worked with anyone but you on these books. Diva move, but whatev. ;) The series wouldn't be *close* to what it is without your Edits of Sparkle, side notes that make me LOL, and serious dedication that you devote to Canterwood.

Ross, two words—Denny Crane.

Jinny Caswell, the scones and funny cat cards fueled my writing. Much love!

Hugs to the amazing readers who keep me going during the final stretch of pages. Special hearts to the guys who have e-mailed to chat about Canterwood—it means a lot to hear from you!

Thanks to Bonne Bell for giving Sasha an endless supply of fave lip glosses.

Thanks so much to all my writer friends who offer support and encouragement. Twirl has to be on when I write, and Tweets from Mandy Morgan, Maggie Stiefvater, Bri, Becca Leach, Lauren Barnholdt, the Canterwood cast, Melissa Walker, Kate Brian, Ally Carter, Ellen Hopkins, and Becca Fitzpatrick always keep me entertained.

K . . . by the time SRL is out, all of this will be *far* behind us and it'll be time to add to your line-art collection. And mine, too. YAMG. ☺ LYSM. <3

DECISIONS, DECISIONS

ONE BOX TO GO.

I kneeled in front of a cardboard box that I'd shoved in the corner of Brit's—well, *our*—room. It was the only box left to open after I'd moved into Orchard Hall two weeks ago. I stared at the scissors in my hand, clenching them and waiting for the chest crush to come when I thought about how I'd moved out of my old room. The space I'd shared with my ex(?)—best friend and roommate, Paige Parker.

But, instead, the sadness was only a twinge. Fourteen days wasn't enough for us to even begin to reevaluate our friendship, but it *was* enough to allow me to realize that I liked living with Brit.

And I was ready to unpack the last box and make this room completely mine, too.

I slid the scissors along the tape at the top of the box and pulled out summer clothes that I hadn't needed to unpack right away since it was mid-October. The tank tops, shorts, and T-shirts fit into the top drawer that Brit had cleared out for me in our dark wooden dresser. I slid the drawer closed and stood back, hands on my hips, surveying the room as *mine* for the first time since I'd moved in.

The room was bigger than my old one and had glossy hardwood floors, a whiteboard with notes written in neon-colored markers, and soft cream-colored eyelet curtains that swayed gently in the breeze through the slightly open windows. Above the window panes, Brit had twinkly star-shaped lights that made the coziest shadows at night. My feet sank into the pink plush carpet and I sat down on my desk chair.

A key turned in the doorknob and Brit, carrying a FedEx box, stepped inside. She looked every inch runway-ready in her tall black boots with skinny jeans tucked into them and a ribbed, plum-colored V-neck sweater. She may have looked it, but Brit wasn't from New York City like many of the students at Canterwood Crest—she was a small-town girl like me. A fact that had definitely fast-tracked our bond.

"Hey, Sash," she said. Her smile brightened her

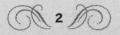

almond-shaped eyes when she looked at me. Her glossy, long black hair was in a side braid.

"Hey, looks like you got the box you were waiting for," I said.

"Yep!" Brit put the box on the floor, nodding. "My parents got us Halloween decorations for our room. Stephanie had them in her office and I almost ripped the box out of her hands."

I laughed, pulling my light brown hair into a loose ponytail. "Halloween *is* our favorite holiday."

"And hello—it's in two weeks!" Brit brushed her bangs out of her eyes. "Since it *is* a Sunday *and* all of our homework is done, want to decorate?"

"Hmmm . . ." I pretended to think about it. "Yes!"

Brit and I kneeled on the floor beside the box and she sliced it open. She pulled out a layer of black and orange tissue paper. Plastic spider confetti sprinkled onto the carpet and we giggled. A note was under the layer of paper.

Brit—Happy Halloween! Dad and I hope you and your new roommate like the decorations. We miss you! Xoxo, Mom and Dad

"Let's see what we've got," Brit said. She reached into the box and started handing me items. There was a giant cardboard cutout skeleton to hang on our door, a set of plastic tombstones with funny names like "Barry A. Live,"

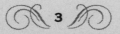

"Reed N. Weep," and "Otta B. Alive." There were two pairs of fake wax fangs and a giant bagful of mixed gum and candy bars. I wanted to dive into the orange M&M's immediately.

Brit handed me a giant rubber spider with an orange sticker that said SQUEEZE ME! on its stomach. I did, making it squeak. Brit and I laughed. I looked at the spider, unable to either stop the flashbacks to last Halloween or stop thinking about how different things were now. Last year, Callie, my ex-BFF, and I had been dressing miniature horses up in costumes for a charity auction. Paige, my other BFF, and I had spent days leading up to Halloween watching funny-slash-scaryish (read: *no* blood!) Halloween movies and eating a ton of candy corn. This year, well, Callie hadn't been a part of my life for a while and that had been painful enough. But now, with the possibility of losing Paige completely, there were moments when I didn't know what to do. But having Brit definitely made things easier.

"Sash, isn't this cool?" Brit handed me a sheet of vinyl window decals. They had jack-o'-lanterns with different faces—some creepy, some silly—plus bats, ghosts, black cats, and a few stars.

"These are so fun. They're going to look great."

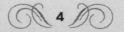

Brit got up and plugged in a pumpkin that looked real. She pushed a button on the cord and a warm glow came out of its eyes, mouth, and nose. It looked perfect on our small end table.

"Love it," I said. "I'm going to start the window clings."

I took a sheet from Brit and pulled up the blinds, letting sunshine filter through the glass. Standing back, I stared at the window, deciding where to place each cling. This was obviously *very* serious. A laughing ghost fit at the corner of the window, angled and looking just right.

Brit and I spent another hour arranging the decorations exactly as we wanted them. We laughed and chatted the entire time as if we'd been BFFs our whole lives. Some days, I'd questioned the decision to move out of my room with Paige and there had been nights that I'd been awake for hours wondering if I'd made the right decision. But now, looking over at Brit and feeling comfortable and stress-free in my own space, I *knew* I'd made the right decision.

"And I think we're done," Brit said. She stepped back and surveyed the room, hands on her hips.

"I think you're right!"

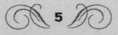

The room was spectacularly spooky with orange, black, and silver in every corner.

I stood, a slight chill making me shiver, and thought about how different this Halloween was going to be from last year.

2

THINGS ARE GOOD

I PULLED ON MY GRAY V-NECK CASHMERE sweater and snuggled into the warm fabric. I wanted to ignore the slight rumble in my stomach, but it was time for dinner. Every dinner, every class still made me feel . . . confused. There was the yummy possibility of seeing Jacob Schwartz, my now official *boyfriend*, but there was also the chance of running into Paige or—even worse—Callie.

"Ready?" Brit asked. She tugged on a pair of black ankle boots over her skinny jeans.

I nodded, my mouth a little dry. Callie and I had spent an *extremely* uneasy two weeks passing each other in the Orchard hallway, sharing classes and eyeing each other in the caf.

Brit studied me. She'd most likely seen this look on my face often enough to know what was wrong. "Sash, it's okay. You're *allowed* to go out. If you run into Callie and she *does* want to talk about your birthday party, it'll probably make things easier. But she hasn't said a word to you yet, so I *really* doubt she's going to bring it up right now."

I took a deep breath. "You're right. I don't think she's ready to talk." *Maybe she'll never talk to me again,* I thought.

"It's time to stop hiding," Brit said. "You live here, we're roommates, Jacob's been amazing, and you've got Charm. Things are *good.*" She smiled, running a brush through her enviably silky black hair. Her almond eyes were a dark brown that complemented her smooth, coffee-colored skin tone. "The Callie sitch *will* work out. Promise."

"You're right." I thought about what she said, letting the words sink in. "Things *are* good."

I slipped my feet into studded black ballet flats and followed Brit out of our room. We closed the door behind us, the wreath of black bats and silver moons lifting my spirits.

"No one else has decorated yet," Brit said as we walked down Orchard's hallway. I loved the cranberry-colored walls that made it feel more like fall than ever. All of the

doors had posters, GO CANTERWOOD CREST ACADEMY flags, or whiteboards. The two-story brick building felt more and more like home every day. We passed the common room, with the gas fireplace blazing. Several of the other Orchard residents studied on the cream-colored couches or the leather recliners. Soon, that would be Brit and me. Canterwood, notorious for tough teachers and insane amounts of homework, would keep us with our books open almost every minute we weren't riding.

Brit pulled out her purple-encased BlackBerry. "Heather just texted me. The Trio's on their way to dinner. Want to sit with them?"

"Definitely," I said. "I know Jacob's at football practice right now, so he won't be there."

Just saying his name made me smile. It gave me that supercliché butterfly feeling.

"Oooh," Brit teased, elbowing me. "Someone's thinking about her boyfriend. Are you imagining kissing him in the courtyard under the moonlight?"

I blushed, laughing. "No! Okay, well, maybe *now* I am."

We giggled and pushed open the glass doors.

The mid-October air was crisp and chilly and I linked arms with Brit for warmth. We walked down the swept, winding sidewalk toward the cafeteria. I'd always had *the*

hardest time deciding if campus was more stunning during fall or winter, but right now, I couldn't stop admiring what was around me.

As a scared seventh grader over a year ago, when I'd first looked at the campus, I'd felt as if I hadn't belonged here. It was as though Canterwood's reputation for not only being a top-notch East Coast boarding school with rigorous academics but also a school known for having a tough equestrian program had made it a place where I shouldn't have been allowed. The small-town girl in me had been overwhelmed by the prestige of the school. I looked over at Brit, watching her look around at the other students milling around the courtyard and heading to dinner.

Brit Chan.

No one would ever be able to tell that she, too, was from a tiny town.

"Hey, Brit," a strawberry-blond girl called.

And there it was.

Unlike my transition, hers had been seamless and she'd become the new It Girl without being mean or vindictive or two-faced girl.

Brit waved back, now having the attention of people sitting on stone benches as we approached. Brit was dangerously close to dethroning the queen of our eighth

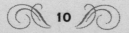

grade—Heather Fox—and I couldn't even begin to guess what a change in regime would mean for our school.

Brit and I kept walking up the sidewalk and I stared ahead, trying not to notice the younger students staring with wide eyes at Brit. Giant trees had dropped most of their orange, red, and yellow leaves, covering the still-green cropped grass. Black iron lampposts lit the darkening walk to the caf and warm lights glowed from different buildings.

"I'm starving," Brit said, pulling open one of the caf's heavy doors.

"Me too."

When we reached the enormous cafeteria, as I'd been doing since my blowout with Paige, I scanned the room before entering.

Whew. I didn't see Callie or Paige.

"Are you planning on moving or have you decided to become a permanent roadblock?"

I jumped, turning at the sound of Heather's voice. Her two BFFs, Julia Myer and Alison Robb, flanked her. The girls smirked.

"You got me," I said. "I decided to just stand here and have my food delivered."

That made Alison smile. Her sandy brown hair was in

soft curls and she looked ready for a dinner *party* instead of a regular Sunday night dinner. She wore thigh-high, camel-colored boots with a matching skirt, sheer tights, and a soft-looking white sweater.

"Let's grab food before we starve while listening to your 'jokes'," Heather said, making air quotes.

I rolled my eyes, but couldn't stop my smile. Heather's biting attitude was nothing new. Plus, we'd become friends since I'd stayed with her during fall break. I'd chosen to stay in Heather's Park Avenue penthouse instead of going home with Paige as I'd originally planned. And now I was still learning how to handle the fallout.

In the line, the five of us grabbed silver trays and got them loaded with steaming rosemary chicken and rice. In the dessert section, I took a small plate and placed a red velvet cupcake on it. The rest of the girls took cupcakes or tarts.

We took our usual table and I sat across from Brit and next to Julia. Even though the cafeteria wasn't one of my top ten places to be right now because of my situation, I still loved being here. The tables—a mix of circular and rectangles—were angled differently throughout the room. My fave part was the giant bay window that gave a spectacular view of campus. Since the caf building was on an incline, it was a great spot to observe all of the activities going on around campus. But with the Trio and Brit, the most interesting part of the campus was what was going on at our table.

"How's Apollo's hoof?" Julia asked. She tucked a piece of her now-longer blond bob behind her ears, and picked up her fork.

Brit smiled at the sound of her horse's name. She'd only been leasing the gray gelding for about six months, but they looked as if they'd been together since Apollo had been broken.

"It's totally healed," Brit said. "I'm still being careful with him and we're not doing anything too rigorous. But Mr. Conner said the vet's coming tomorrow to give him another checkup and, hopefully, clear us to get back to a regular training schedule."

"Alison and I have to get more time in the arena," Julia said. "I mean, I guess we got lucky that Mr. Nicholson got sick and couldn't make our YENT testing two weeks ago, but . . .

"Now we've got an extra two weeks to worry," she finished. She shoved rice around on her plate. She *never* acted worried about riding. But the YENT, or Youth Equestrian National Team, was the goal for every rider at

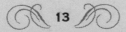

Canterwood who dreamed of making it big on the show circuit—maybe even to the Olympics.

"We'd already have either been on the team or been told 'no' a long time ago if *Jasmine* hadn't been involved," Alison said, making a face.

I almost shivered depsite my warm clothes. Jasmine King, a former Wellington Prep student, had transferred to Canterwood—set to take out the Trio, Callie, and me. Jas had framed Julia and Alison, making it seem as if they'd cheated on a history exam. Thanks to Jasmine, they'd been kicked off the riding team and had missed their chance at the YENT. But their chance was coming. In two weeks.

"Enough talk about that Wellington witch," Heather said, rolling her blue eyes. She'd dusted shimmery white powder in the corners of her eyes and it made her look even more tan—despite the fact that it was October.

"Agreed," we all said, nodding.

"How are things with Jacob?" Heather asked.

She'd been the one who'd pushed us together—admittedly, by extreme means—over fall break. Heather had e-mailed Jacob all during break, pretending she was me. But it had been the push I'd unknowingly needed. After break, I'd met him in the courtyard and we decided we'd

never had a shot at a real relationship. We had too much history to throw away everything now that we were both single—and unable to stay away from each other.

"We've been IMing, texting, and talking a lot," I said. "I think . . . he's going to ask me on a date soon."

"Omigosh!" Alison said, clapping. "It's about time. We've been back to school two weeks, so he *better* ask you on a date."

"Ben and I are catching a movie tonight," Julia said. "We've been together forever and it's the first chance we've had time to go out since we got back to school."

Heather nodded. "Things have been crazy. Troy and I . . ."

Heather stopped for a second, trailing off.

"What's going on with you and Troy?" Brit asked. Her tone was gentle, not pressing.

I'd filled her in on how I'd managed to convince Heather to talk to Troy—her long-time crush—during fall break. Heather rarely let her front down, the act of being an alpha clique leader, but I'd seen her vulnerable side during fall break. She was afraid of rejection from guys she *really* liked, even though she went after (and got) almost every boy on campus.

"Troy and I are taking things slow," Heather said.

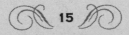

"We texted earlier and we're going to groom our horses together tomorrow after lessons."

"That sounds perf," Alison said. "You'll be super-comfortable in the stable. It's the place you've seen each other the most before you even started like-liking each other."

"That does sound great," I said. "The weather's supposed to be nice, so maybe tie the horses up near one of the pastures and get away from everyone."

Heather took a bite of chicken. "That's not, like, a horrible idea."

For the rest of dinner, the Trio, Brit, and I talked about boys, riding, and classes. Our easy chatter and laughter made me forget to be on the lookout for Paige and Callie.

3

INTO THE RABBIT HOLE

ON MONDAY MORNING, I SAT DOWN IN MR.
Davidson's English class. His advanced class was one of
my favorites—only ten students were in the class. Paige
was one of them. I thought back to the moment we'd
found out we'd been accepted to the accelerated English
class. Not allowing myself to pause, I walked through the
door and sat in my usual seat among the comfy chairs
arranged in a circle. No one else was in the classroom yet.

I opened my silver, sparkly notebook and dated a fresh
piece of paper for notes. We were starting a new book
today—*Alice's Adventures in Wonderland*. I opened my copy,
and flipped through the pages. A total bookworm, I'd
been wanting to read this forever.

The classroom door opened and I looked up, seeing

Paige enter. Our eyes met and I was sure her smile mirrored mine. Paige sat across from me, opening her leather messenger bag. She pulled out her book, notebook, and a pen.

"Hi." My voice, though soft, sounded as if it came out through a cheerleader's megaphone.

"Hey," Paige said. She pulled her hair over one shoulder, one of her nervous telltales.

A sadness passed between us—we were still so close that I could feel it. And just like every other class we'd had together since I'd moved out of Winchester Hall, Paige and I sat in silence until the classroom filled. Alison, one of the last students to arrive, took a chair two seats down from me and smiled at me, obviously trying to show empathy for my situation with Paige.

"Morning everyone," Mr. Davidson said, taking his seat. He had a dog-eared copy of *Alice* filled with sticky notes in his hand and a clipboard with stapled handouts.

We all greeted him back.

"I'd like you all to pass around these sheets for *Alice*," Mr. Davidson said, handing them to Vanessa Ortiz. She handed them to the next person and we passed them around. "This is your syllabus for our latest read. You'll find some quiz dates, essay topics and due dates, and the first homework assignment."

"You said '*some* quiz dates'," a guy name Aaron said.

Mr. Davidson nodded, pulling glasses down from his dark blond hair. "Meaning there will still be pop quizzes."

There was a collective groan in the class, causing Mr. Davidson to smile. "C'mon, guys," he said. "There will only be a few—promise."

I flipped through the syllabus, trying not to freak myself out over the workload. This was an advanced class, and I'd come in knowing it would require a lot of time, but the syllabus for the time we were spending on *Alice* was L-O-N-G. *At least it's a book you're superinterested in.*

"Let's talk briefly about the plot," Mr. Davidson said. "Has anyone read the book, or watched the Disney movie? What do you know about it?"

Alison raised her hand, and Mr. Davidson nodded at her. "I've only seen the movie. A girl falls down a well, meets a crazy guy—the Mad Hatter—and tries not to have her head chopped off by the Queen of Hearts."

I nodded, raising my hand. "I watched the movie a while ago. I remember the Cheshire Cat and the Caterpillar."

"I'm glad not all of you are familiar with the movie," Mr. Davidson said. "We're going to hold a screening of it after we finish the book. It will be part of your final assignment—to compare and contrast the two. " He

looked at Alison and me. "Both of you will find that the book and movie are *quite* different."

And that was one reason why Mr. Davidson was one of my fave teachers. Watching *Alice* after reading was something to look forward to after a grueling schedule while reading and writing.

I walked across campus, shifting my heavy Steve Madden (hello, Macy's sale!) shoulder bag from one arm to the next. The rest of my classes had been fine, but I was *so* ready for lunch. My phone buzzed in my backpack. I unzipped the pocket, pulling out my new BlackBerry. I'd managed to convince my parents to let me upgrade my ancient phone last week so I could BlackBerry Message with the Trio, Brit, and my other friends from school.

I opened BBM and found a message waiting from Jacob.

Want to sit together at lunch? Something to ask you.

I typed back. *Sure! See you at the caf.* ☺

I switched to my convo with Brit. *Sitting w/Jacob @ lunch. He's going to ask me something!*

I watched my phone as I walked, seeing Brit type back.

He's totally gonna ask you on a date.

I reread her message three times before responding.

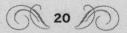

I really, REALLY don't know. But hopefully . . . will BBM u after.

Brit typed back the thumbs-up emoticon.

I put my phone back in my bag, trying not to let my knees wobble as I entered the cafeteria. Turning my head, I looked for Jacob. We saw each at the same time and looking at him made me smile the way I did when I looked only at him.

His brown hair contrasted with his eyes—making the green look almost emerald. I weaved through the other students, not even hearing the chatter as I made my way to him.

"Hey," we said simultaneously.

I giggled, and then groaned silently for sounding like a silly, boy-crazed girl. I was more than into trying again with Jacob and I couldn't stop thinking about him, but riding was still my top priority. As Jacob and I tried out our new relationship, I'd have to find a balance between my fave guys—Jacob and Charm. At least Charm, my Thoroughbred-Belgian gelding, liked Jacob.

"So you have something to ask me, huh?" I said, unable to stop myself from blurting it out.

Jacob smiled. "Oh, just something. Let's grab food and find a quiet table."

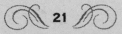

I could barely stand it. I wanted to know right *now* what he wanted to ask me. What if it wasn't what I thought at all? Maybe it had nothing to do with a date. It could be something dumb. Maybe he was going to ask me if I *had* to carry eight lip glosses in my bag at all times. Or maybe he was going to ask me if I could tutor him in English—his weakest subject.

Racing through the lunch line, I put Thai food on my tray in a kind of sloppy mess. Green curry with chicken, sticky rice, and a nectarine for dessert. I grabbed chopsticks, something I was still mastering, from the bin and waited for Jacob. He'd picked red curry, basil fried rice, and egg rolls. Jacob nabbed a bowl of chocolate pudding and we both put Diet Cokes on our trays.

"How about that table?" Jacob asked. He jerked his chin in the direction of a table for two in the back corner by the window.

"Perfect."

I forced myself to keep pace with Jacob and not race ahead of him, even though I wanted to snag our table, slam down my tray and beg him to tell me what he wanted to ask me.

But that's sooo desperate, I told myself. *You can wait. Just chill.*

The time it took us to walk across the cafeteria

seemed to take forever, but within seconds, we were seated on the caf chairs. I twisted off the cap of my Diet Coke and Jacob did the same. Sipping it, I waited for him to say something first. Under the table, my foot jiggled.

"How's everything so far today?" Jacob asked.

Arrrgh! So he wasn't going to ask me right *this second!*

"Good," I said. "We're reading a book I'm excited about in English and I'm glad it's lunchtime. And I'm ready for classes to be over soon and to go riding."

Jacob took a bite of steaming hot curry. "Same about wanting classes to be over. Math was brutal today. But it's okay—the day's more than half over and Mondays are always long."

"Sorry about math. Yeah, Mondays suck, but you're right. We *are* almost done for the day."

Jacob popped a cherry tomato into his mouth and I forced myself to eat a bite of rice. Green curry was my new fave Thai food, but I wasn't interested in the food. All I wanted was for Jacob to tell me what he'd BBMed me about.

Jacob put down his fork, and took a looong sip of his Diet Coke. "Not hungry?" he asked, gesturing at my plate.

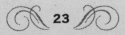

23

"No, I'm hungry, I just—" I stopped when I caught the teasing tone in his voice.

Jacob gave me a teasing smile. "I know you, Sash."

I blushed. "Okay, I *might* be a *tiny* bit curious about what you said. Just a little."

Jacob reached across the table, outstretching his hand palm up. I placed my hand in his and his larger fingers closed over mine. I was glad I'd showered this morning and slathered my rein-roughed hands with Origins lotion. The fresh grapefruit scent made me happy every time I wore it. Now I took a breath, trying to slow my breathing.

"I wanted to wait a couple of weeks until we both got used to school before I asked you this," Jacob said. "But things have settled down with classes and, well, everything. Sasha, do you have plans for Wednesday?"

"No! Nope! Nothing!" *Omigod! Shut up!* I screamed at myself. I didn't have to answer him so quickly.

Jacob squeezed my hand, laughing. "I'm glad. I was hoping you'd be free so that we could go out. On our first date."

A date with Jacob was something I'd been dreaming about from the day I'd first seen him at Canterwood, except for when I'd been with Eric, my ex-boyfriend.

"I'd really, really like to go out with you on Wednesday." I squeezed his hand, warmth passing between our hands.

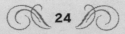

"I'll pick you up at seven, okay?" Jacob asked.

"Perfect," I said, my voice a little high.

We let go of each other's hands and went back to our lunches. I scanned the room, looking for Brit, and I saw her sitting with the Trio. A BBM convo with Brit about my talk Jacob wasn't even necessary. With one look at me, she knew. Brit grinned and immediately turned to Heather, covering her mouth with her hands to whisper to the Trio what had just happened. And one by one, the Trio—even Julia—smiled at me. There was an extra ounce of sparkle in Heather's eyes—she understood more than anyone about The Jacob Thing.

After lunch, Jacob and I agreed to IM later and I stared after him when he walked away.

Within seconds, Brit was at my side. "Oh my God," she said. "Tell me everything."

I didn't even pause for a second. "Jacob said he'd been waiting for the right time for things to settle down and things finally felt good. He asked if I had any plans for Wednesday and, like a crazy rambling person, I said no *three* times."

Brit laughed. "Well, you were just making sure that he understood that you were free."

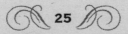

I covered my face with my hands. "He *definitely* knows for sure. I was sure a dork!"

Brit and I left the caf and she shook her head. "You were just excited. I would have acted the same way—trust me."

The smile I'd had all though lunch faltered a little when I couldn't help but think about one person.

Paige. Sure, she'd been the one who'd told the whole truth about Jacob kissing me at my birthday party to Callie, but she would have been the first one I'd told about the date before I moved out. And now, my space was occupied by Geena—Paige's close friend from cooking class. I was torn between feeling a strange sense of loss and one of happiness that Paige wasn't alone in my former room. I couldn't be a hypocrite—I *did* have Brit. Plus, Paige deserved and needed to have someone there.

I just couldn't even comprehend what had gone through Paige's mind when she and Callie had talked.

"What's wrong?" Brit asked. "You look sad."

"Just thinking about Paige," I said. "I mean, we used to be best friends. I don't know anything that's going on in her life and that seems so weird. "

We kept walking toward Orchard, keeping a steady pace since we had a riding lesson in a while.

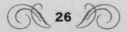

"I had a messy split with my old best friend," Brit said. She shifted her backpack, getting out the keys to our room.

"What happened?"

"We were BFFs for years and she was always *super* supportive of my riding. She wasn't into sports, but she got that I loved horses and wanted to spend time at the stable riding and being around horses."

I stepped around a clump of leaves that had blown onto the sidewalk. "What happened? I mean, you totally don't have to talk about it, if it's uncomfortable."

Brit half smiled. "No, it's okay. It happened a couple of years ago and I still miss her, but it might make you feel better about Paige."

Brit opened the door to Orchard and we stepped inside the busy hallway. Everyone was getting back from classes now. A lot of doors were open so friends could walk back and forth from each other's rooms and gossip about the day.

Brit and I walked to our room and she unlocked the door. We tossed our heavy bags on the floor and kicked off our shoes.

"So, my old best friend, Karlie, got interested in boys and started hanging out with this really popular girl, Justine, at our school. Karlie and I were *never* popular, but

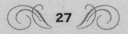

after Justine wanted to be her friend, Karlie almost acted as if we'd never met before."

"Omigod," I said. I pulled fawn-colored breeches, a pair of brown paddock boots, and a long-sleeve shirt from my closet. "That's horrible. I get the whole sudden-interest-in-boys thing, I really do, but there's *no* excuse for dropping your best friend."

Brit pulled a V-neck, sky blue shirt over her head. "I know. She just stopped texting or calling. We used to have sleepovers every weekend and tell each other *everything*. Then, she just got bored with my riding schedule."

"Did you guys ever talk about it?" I asked.

"She wouldn't even talk to me about it at school," Brit said. "I finally called her cell one night and she answered. She said I was just too busy for her, which wasn't true, and that Justine was a really great girl." Brit shook her head. "She left out the fact that Justine was the meanest girl in our grade."

"Ohhh no," I said, lacing up a paddock boot.

"Yup." Brit shut her closet door harder than usual. "I know Paige didn't do that, but I remember what it felt like not to hear her ringtone anymore or spend nights at her house or know silly things like if her little sister was being bratty."

"That's how I feel," I said. "I'm happy Paige has Geena—I really, *really* am. But I can't stop wondering how things are with her. Like, what's going on with Ryan? Their relationship is so new. Is he still being a good guy to her? And what about her grades? And her parents? And . . ." I took a breath, pausing during my rambling.

"And what?" Brit's tone was soft. She combed her long hair into a low ponytail that would fit under her helmet.

I reached for my Rosebud strawberry lip balm. "And, I don't know, does she miss me?"

Brit walked over, touching my shoulder. "I'm sure she does, Sasha. Thing will settle down, you'll see. It's just going to take time, but things will work out. In the meantime, you've got a lot to keep you busy and so does she."

I finished tying my other boot and got off our chair. "Thanks, Brit. That made me feel a lot better. I know we'll talk when we're both ready."

I brushed back my own hair, then grabbed my phone. "Shall we?"

"Let's."

Brit and I smiled at each other, leaving our room for the stables. There was no one I wanted to see more than Charm right now. Just thinking about his sweet face and giant brown eyes made me feel like I could get through anything.

4
BEYOND MAJOR

BRIT AND I GOT TO THE STABLE WITH PLENTY OF time to spare before our lesson. Lateness was one of the many things Mr. Conner didn't tolerate. He kicked out riders who weren't in the arena on time and it was something that terrified me even now.

Brit and I walked to the tack room, tossing around ideas about what we'd be doing in class.

"I *so* hope it's dressage," Brit said. "But I need to work on jumping, too."

"I'm the opposite," I said, laughing. "I really should be working on dressage more, though—it's my weakest area. But Charm and I sooo heart jumping."

Brit pushed open the tack room door. Eric, bridle over his shoulder, was inside, gathering Luna's tack.

"Hey," I said.

"Hi, guys," Eric said to Brit and me.

After fall break, Eric and I had talked. We'd decided we didn't want to avoid each other all year. Canterwood was stressful enough. We'd even talked about practicing together soon, or trail riding when we got burned out. Our friendship was still new, but Eric was the kind of guy who was naturally, genuinely kind. He always made me feel comfortable and I still felt as if I could call him in the middle of the night if I ever needed him. But maybe that had been part of the problem—I liked Eric too much as a friend. With Jacob, there had always been boyfriend/girlfriend chemistry between us.

"How's Luna?" I asked.

"Perfect," Eric said, a smile on his light brown face. "We've been especially in sync the past few days. She's moving well and really listening to me."

"That's great!" I said. "I definitely want to watch sometime."

Eric loved Luna, the flea-bitten gray mare he rode. She was Canterwood's horse, but Eric was the one who rode her the most. Though he wasn't on the YENT, Eric was an extremely talented rider who was on his way to one day making the YENT. If he'd had the opportunities that

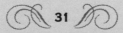

Callie, Alison, and Julia had, he would have been testing with them on Wednesday.

"Maybe we can all practice together soon," Eric said, extending his smile toward Brit.

"Definitely," she said. "Our horses haven't officially met yet."

Eric brushed his black hair from his eyes. "That's true. We'll all have to text and figure out a day." He lifted Luna's saddle pad and English saddle onto his arm. "See you later."

Brit and I waved bye, watching his back until he shut the tack room door.

"He definitely seems as nice as you've told me," Brit said. "It'll be fun to ride with him sometime."

"For sure." I rubbed my finger over Charm's snaffle bit. "He *is* a great guy. Even after our breakup, he wasn't a jerk." I gathered Charm's tack. "Do you think we should invite Rachel to ride with us?"

"Is Eric dating her?" Brit asked, referring to the seventh grader Eric had been hanging out with a lot.

"It seems like it," I said. "I don't know if it's casual or serious, but I guess we should think about inviting her."

I thought back to how I'd *despised* Rachel and her friends when I'd been with Eric. She'd been crushing on

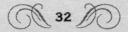

him and even though I'd trusted Eric completely, Rachel had made me jealous. Embarrassingly jealous.

Brit and I walked down the aisle and she reached Apollo's stall first. The friendly gray gelding had his head poked over the stall door, almost seeming to want to push out the stall door when he saw Brit.

"See you in the arena," I said.

I hurried down the aisle toward Charm's stall, weaving around horses in crossties and groups of riders chatting between classes. If I could, I'd spend all day with Charm. It wasn't just about riding for me—I loved everything about horses from caring for them to learning about nutrition. I dreamed about opening my own stable after college and after . . . the Olympics.

But first, I had to prove myself on the YENT.

"Hi, gorgeous!" I said to Charm as soon as I saw his copper-colored head with its white blaze over the door, reaching for me. I put down his tack, unlatched his stall door, and closed it behind me. One-on-one time was our thing before a lesson.

I wrapped my arms around his neck. I had to stand on tiptoe to reach him, he was so tall. Charm's always-clean chestnut coat gleamed from his daily grooming.

"How are you doing today?" I asked, rubbing his cheek.

I ran my finger over the gold nameplate on his dark brown leather halter. "Ready for a lesson?"

Charm, obviously able to understand certain words, nodded at "lesson."

"Good," I said. "Because I have a feeling that it's going to be a tough one today."

Holding on to Charm's halter, I led him out of his stall and deciding to skip crossties, used a slip-knot to secure his lead line to bars on his stall. Sometimes, it was just nice to stay out of the craziness of the stable before a lesson. It gave me time to calm down after school before jumping into another intense activity.

I opened Charm's lacquered wooden trunk and pulled out his grooming box. He wasn't dirty, so I skipped the dandy brush and grabbed his blue body brush. Charm leaned into my brush strokes as I started at his poll and moved down his neck. He was just starting to grow a winter coat. In a couple of months, he'd be fuzzy, even though I blanketed him during every turnout.

The stable chatter got louder as I moved the brush across his withers—lightly flicking dust from him. After his coat was clean, I took his wide-toothed comb and ran it through his trimmed mane and tail.

My mind started to wander as I thought about Jacob

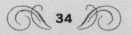

and our date. What would I wear? Normally, that was something Paige and I would obsess over together. *But,* I reminded myself, *Brit is just as chic as Paige. She won't let me go on my first date with Jacob looking like an idiot.*

"Are you trying to bald him?"

"Huh?" I said, looking up.

Heather, holding a tacked-up Aristocrat's reins, looked at me. Troy stood next to her and shot me a smile.

"Our lesson starts in ten," Heather said. "You better be in there on time, Silver. I'm not waiting for you."

Ooops!

"I won't be late," I said. "Why don't you go before *you're* late?"

Heather just smoothed her sky blue shirt that matched her eyes. "Arena. Nine minutes."

"See you, Sasha," Troy said as they walked away.

For a second, I watched them. Heather was starting her first relationship and Troy was perfect for her. A rider, smart and funny—he was the guy for Heather. It had taken a lot of prodding to convince her to text him to say hi over fall break. But once she had, they'd started chatting more and more. I'd even seen them talking over steaming mugs of hot chocolate at The Sweet Shoppe.

Charm snorted, almost as if he was reminding me about the time.

"Right!" I said. "Tacking you up now."

Being careful but with one eye on the big wall clock, I hurried through getting Charm ready and snapped on my black helmet. Charm walked beside me. He knew we were going for a lesson. He pulled on the reins, eager to get to the arena, and stepped ahead of me.

"Hey," I said. "Take it easy."

I pulled on the reins, slowing my own pace, and forcing Charm back beside me. His Thoroughbred blood made him a little overexcited sometimes and he was still a relatively young horse for the type of work we were doing.

Charm listened to me and fell back into place beside me, walking quietly. We reached the massive indoor arena and I halted him. Calm now, he stood still when I slid my left boot into the stirrup and lifted myself into the saddle.

I kept him at a walk and we made our way to the wall. Brit and Heather, already warming up, were trotting their horses. Heather took Aristocrat, her Thoroughbred gelding, through serpentines and while Brit posted as Apollo worked at a collected trot. Charm tossed his head, his mane flying. He pulled on the bit, wanting to catch up to the other horses that were on the other side of the arena.

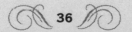

I did a half-halt like Kim, my first instructor, had taught me. I made Charm stay at a walk. He couldn't get away with doing whatever he wanted or he'd never listen to me. When we'd made a complete circle around the arena at a walk, I let him into a trot. He jumped forward, trying to break into a canter, when he saw Apollo only a few strides ahead of him.

"Charm," I said, my voice low. I pulled him back to a walk, causing him to shake his head. It was going to be one of those lessons where I couldn't lose focus for a second. *That* wasn't going to be easy since my mind wanted to be thinking about Jacob.

And his smile.

And his eyes, that were a sparkly green when he looked at me.

And . . .

Mr. Conner walked into the arena. I sat deeper in the saddle and guided Charm to the center of the arena. Brit and Heather rode up too, and we halted in front of Mr. Conner.

He wore his regular riding gear—a hunter green shirt with CCA's logo stitched in gold, tall black boots, and breeches. I felt Charm settle beneath me. He was still intimidated by Mr. Conner too.

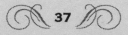

"Good afternoon, everyone," Mr. Conner said.

Heather, Brit, and I nodded at him.

Mr. Conner tucked his clipboard under one elbow as he folded his arms. "We have a lot of work to get through today, but I want to speak with you first."

In my place between Brit and Heather, I glanced quickly at each of them. They both had the same *I don't know what's going on* looks on their faces.

Mr. Conner smiled at us. "There's nothing wrong and no one's in trouble," he said, obviously catching our worried glances.

I relaxed a little, but not much. Whenever Mr. Conner addressed us, there was always an important reason.

"You all performed incredibly well at the schooling show," Mr. Conner said. "It was a great warm-up to the show season."

Thinking about the show made me proud to be part of Canterwood's YENT team. We'd performed well together and had rallied around Brit when Apollo had gotten injured. The bruised hoof had brought Heather, Brit, and me closer and I'd spent a lot of hours helping Brit ice Apollo's hoof and walk him in the cushy grass in the big back pasture.

"Before Thanksgiving break," Mr. Conner said. "There

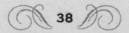

will be a show at Huntington Stables—the Huntington Classic."

Huntington? The word reverberated in my brain. The grounds, only a few hours away, were legendary for hosting qualifying shows. Just being able to say you rode at Huntington was an honor.

"As I'm sure you know," Mr. Conner said. "Riding at your level at Huntington is by invite only." Mr. Conner paused, looking at each of us for a second.

"I'm proud and pleased to announce that you have all been invited to show at Huntington for Canterwood Crest's YENT team before Thanksgiving break," Mr. Conner said.

"But . . ." Brit said, shaking her head. "How? Apollo and I didn't even finish our jumping class at the schooling show."

"The committee at Huntington doesn't just pay attention to a rider's performance at one show," Mr. Conner said. "They choose to invite teams who perform well on a consistent basis. Even though you've all only ridden together once, your individual performances have been taken into consideration whenever you've performed."

"Wow," Brit said, obviously ecstatic.

"Are we scheduling extra practices?" Heather asked.

Mr. Conner nodded. "We're going back to morning *and* afternoon lessons. I don't want anyone or their horses to be pushed, so on some days we will either do morning or afternoon lessons. If you want to practice more, your hours to be in the stable riding will be extended, but I have to clear your request first."

Heather stiffened in the saddle. I knew she hated that new rule. She practiced, almost to the point of overworking herself and Aristocrat, on a regular basis. When shows were involved, she practically lived in the arena.

"If you have questions, please ask now or come find me any time," Mr. Conner said. He held up three envelopes. "These are copies of permission slips that will be sent to your parents. It also explains an important aspect of the Huntington Classic that I've yet to mention."

My heartbeat sped up. Brit, Heather, and I looked at each other again. Hello, potential whiplash!

"There will be seven other YENT teams competing at the Classic," Mr. Conner said. "Individual riders will be rewarded for their performances and their points will be added together for a team score."

P-R-E-S-S-U-R-E.

I clenched my fingers around the reins, trying to keep my breathing steady. I'd known since I'd made the YENT

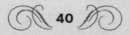

that my score would affect my teammates. But now, at the *Huntington Classic*, it suddenly felt like a bigger deal than ever.

Mr. Conner seemed to be watching us carefully with his dark eyes, judging our reactions. "The three YENT teams who score the highest in your level will receive an incredible honor—an invite to the Essex Fall Show."

I thought I was going to slip from Charm's saddle. First Huntington. Now Essex. These were shows I'd watched on DVD since I was a kid. Now I was competing in one with a shot at competing in the other.

"Wow," I said, my voice barely above a whisper.

Mr. Conner smiled. "Please keep in mind that this is all far off in the future and we don't want to become a team that is only focused on showing. We will still maintain our level of dedication to horse care, nutrition, and most of all, love of riding—not just showing."

Love of riding was something I never worried about losing.

"One more item in the letter," Mr. Conner said. "Is to inform your parents that if—and please try not to immediately begin to focus on this—you perform well at Huntington and Essex, Canterwood's YENT team will have a chance at going to nationals in the spring."

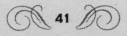

I almost choked.

Mr. Conner raised his hand. "I did *not* want to bombard you with all of this information so early in the show season, but your parents had to be informed about possible traveling and how it would affect your school schedule."

"We can *so* do this!" Heather said. Her confidence was infectious. It made me grin and Brit nodded.

"I really think we can," Brit said. "We're going to work hard, Mr. Conner."

"We won't disappoint you," I added.

Mr. Conner's smile was soft. "None of you are ever disappointments to me. I know you will all work hard, but I want you to maintain your grades, keep seeing your friends, and remember that showing isn't everything. Yes, this is all important for your careers as riders. But I want you all to enjoy yourselves, too, and reward yourselves for the work you've already done and will do in the future."

We nodded. And no matter how exciting (and terrifying!) all of these show dates were, I knew I wasn't going to give up the balance I'd just found with school, friends, and riding. Plus, Jacob and I were just starting a relationship. I wasn't going to give up my second chance with Jacob. But

that didn't mean I'd jeopardize my riding career. I could juggle everything—I knew it.

"And now that I've told you, oh, just a little bit of information—" Mr. Conner said, his tone teasing. "—ready to get started?"

"Yes!" we all answered.

WHO WILL WIN
THE PRIZE?

STILL REELING FROM MR. CONNER'S announcement and the grueling lesson we'd just had, I eased Charm toward the arena wall. We were behind Aristocrat and in front of Apollo.

Aristocrat, a chestnut darker than Charm, was Charm's ex-archnemesis. Charm and Aristocrat had hated each other until Heather and I had become friends. The two horses had seemed to sense that the tension had dissipated between Heather and me. It had only helped our team that Heather, Brit, and I were all friends.

We all dismounted and the second Mr. Conner left the arena, we let out girly squeals—even the never-impressed-by-anything Heather.

"Omigod, omigod," I said. "I can't believe it! We

actually might be traveling! This is really, really it. These shows are *huge*."

We started to lead the horses in lazy circles around the arena to cool them down.

"Don't think about the names of the shows, Silver," Heather said. "Or you'll probably faint."

I rolled my eyes. "Please."

"Guys, this *is* big," Brit said. "But I think Mr. Conner's right—we can't focus on all of the shows at once. We have to take them one at a time. If we don't, we'll miss the excitement of one show because we're already looking forward to the next."

Surprisingly, Heather nodded. "You're right."

And *that* was a phrase I'd never heard Heather Fox utter. I almost wanted to mark the date and time that she told someone else they were right.

We walked the horses until they were cool and started to lead them in opposite directions. The three of us were silent as we walked the horses.

"But we *do* have one thing to keep in mind," Heather called to Brit and me. We stopped and turned, looking at her.

"Jasmine."

● ● ●

I blocked out Heather's parting words as I groomed Charm, put a light blanket on him, and turned him out in the pasture. He deserved a break outside since the weather was nice and Mike had promised to bring him in before nightfall.

I walked past the outdoor arena, stopping as I watched Mr. Conner coach three riders in the arena.

Callie, Julia, and Alison were all cantering their horses around Mr. Conner. He was prepping them for Wednesday's YENT testing.

Callie and Black Jack caught my attention first. The black gelding, always attentive to Callie, moved well under her. They crossed across the arena and he did a flying lead change without a second of hesitation.

Even from yards away, I could see the look of serious determination on Julia's face. She'd pinned her blond hair back and her lips were pressed together. She thumped her heels into Trix's sides and the bay mare leapt forward.

"Julia!" Mr. Conner called.

Julia eased Trix to a walk, then a halt. She ducked her head, already knowing she'd done the wrong thing.

"There's no reason to use your heels that hard," Mr. Conner said. "If you push Trix like that again, you're sitting out the rest of the lesson. Understand?"

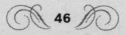

Julia's face blushed Bubble Yum pink. "Yes, sir," she said.

"Please try again," Mr. Conner said. He folded his arms and his eyes followed Julia as she gently urged her compact mare into a trot, then a canter. This time, her movements were soft and when she reached the center of the arena, she signaled Trix to change leads. The mare seemed to freeze for a second, then did as Julia asked.

Julia cantered her to the other side of the arena. She patted Trix's neck, but frowned. I'd seen this superintense side of Julia before. If she didn't rein it in she'd get over-stressed and mess up at YENT trials—I just knew it.

"Alison," Mr. Conner called. "Go ahead."

Out of all of the horses, I adored watching Alison's palomino Arabian move. Sunstruck almost seemed to dance across the arena. His slender legs moved as if he was dancing. Alison, the quietest of the Trio, was the perfect match for her hot-blooded horse. She had the ability to almost predict his spooks and calm him when he became flighty. The seventeen-hand high gelding trusted Alison, and it showed. Not many riders at Canterwood would be able to keep him calm, much less ride him well.

Alison let Sunstruck into a floating trot that moved into a canter. His hoofbeats were barely audible as they

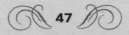

hit the dirt arena. Sunstruck and Alison approached the center of the arena. And, just like the two riders before her, Alison pulled off a beautiful flying lead change.

I started away from the area before Callie, Julia, and Alison knew I'd been watching their lesson. There was no rule that I couldn't, but I understood that they'd want privacy when doing such an important practice. I knew I would.

As I walked back toward Orchard, I shoved my hands in the pockets of my jacket. All three girls were amazing riders. But I had a gut feeling who would make the YENT. I just *knew.*

6

NOW OR NEVER

"READY TO GO, SASH?" BRIT ASKED.

"One sec," I said, heading for my nightstand. "Need my phone."

Brit and I were dressed in regular clothes—not riding clothes—and it felt weird to be on our way to the stable in jeans and sneakers instead of our gear. But we weren't riding. We were going to watch. And after testing, I'd be back in our room to get ready for my *date* with Jacob. Thankfully, there was YENT testing to watch otherwise I'd be counting the seconds till seven when Jacob was picking me up.

Wednesday was finally here and in minutes, Callie, Julia, and Alison were going to be in the arena in front of Mr. Nicholson. Callie had already experienced riding in front of him and had been distracted by Jacob. He'd been dating her then and Callie had lost focus in the weeks before testing—not practicing or focusing on work that needed to be done with Jack. But after what I'd seen yesterday, I knew she was ready.

Unfortunately for my ex–best friend, so were Julia and Alison. I'd texted them an hour ago to say good luck. Alison had written back *THANK YOU!!* and I hadn't heard from Julia. Not that I'd expected to— she'd probably already been practicing or had her phone turned off.

Brit and I left Orchard, heading for the stables. There was a cool breeze in the air and I wrapped sweater-clad arms across my chest. Brit shivered and zipped her PINK hoodie with a white heart on the back.

"I remember exactly how I felt before my YENT test," Brit said. "I was freaking out. Mr. Nicholson and the rest of the scouts were so nice, but I couldn't stop being nervous."

"How many riders were testing with you?" I asked.

"Six," Brit said. "And we already had one YENT rider in my grade, so I thought my chances were really slim."

The wind blew strands of hair out of my ponytail and they stuck in my Urban Decay XXX Shine gloss.

"Well, you obviously did a great job," I said. "Because you made the team."

Brit, modest, shrugged. "I did the best I could and I guess it was enough for Mr. Nicholson. He told me the next day that I made the team and, oh my God, it was so embarrassing."

"What? Why?"

"I started crying!" Brit laughed, covering her face. "Seriously embarrassing."

We laughed together as we walked down the sloped hill to the stables. Students were everywhere. Everyone wanted to watch YENT tryouts, even though Mr. Conner had already posted a note that anyone who wasn't already on the YENT couldn't watch from inside the arena. They'd have to watch in the stands by the outdoor arena for the jumping round. No one but YENT judges were allowed on the cross-country course.

I flashed back to my YENT tryout with Callie, Jasmine, and Heather. My parents and Eric had been in the stands cheering me on. Jacob had been there too, cheering on Callie—or so I thought. But he'd really been there for me. Charm and I had sweated our way through dressage, raced over the cross-country course, and jumped through a good round in the arena.

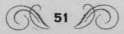

It felt so weird to be going to sit in the indoor skybox to watch the dressage round. It felt like I should be the one who was being tested. Half the time, I still didn't believe I was on the YENT.

Brit and I walked through the back entrance of the indoor arena and up the stairs to the skybox.

"I'm nervous and I'm not even riding," Brit said.

"I know, me too."

We opened the door and Heather was already seated. Mr. and Mrs. Harper, Mr. Robb and Mr. and Mrs. Myer were all in the front row, peering down at their daughters. Alison had said Mrs. Robb had the flu, and I didn't see her there. Callie's parents looked up at me and gave me a brief smile. They'd been nice whenever I'd met them, but Callie had obviously told them about our nonexistent friendship. I gave them a polite smile back.

Brit and I took a seat next to Heather, whose eyes followed two-thirds of the Trio warming up in the arena.

"How does everyone look?" I asked her.

"Good," Heather said, her eyes not leaving the arena. "Sunstruck was a little jumpy at the beginning of the warm-up, but Alison anticipated that. She started working him early to wear him down a little."

"And Julia?" Brit asked.

I looked at Heather's lap, noting that her hands were clasped together and her knuckles were almost white. Testing hadn't even started yet.

"Julia's tight," Heather said, keeping her voice low. She probably didn't want any of the parents to hear. "She's got to relax. I told her before that she needed to chill or she was going to make Trix nervous. There are only a few minutes of warm-up left, so I hope she calms down by then."

I settled my gaze on Callie and Black Jack. Callie's boots gleamed against white breeches. She wore her best black show jacket and a white collared shirt. Black Jack looked just as put together—his shiny trimmed coat made him look supersleek and his movements were loose.

"How's—" I started to ask.

"Callie's amazing," Heather said, knowing what I wanted to ask. "She's been cool the entire warm-up. I was grooming Aristocrat when she got here and she tacked up Black Jack outside Aristocrat's stall. You couldn't even tell she was testing today by watching her."

But I knew Callie. This day—the next few hours—meant everything to her. It was her chance to reclaim what she really did deserve—a spot on the YENT with Brit, Heather, and me. My stomach tightened and I took a deep breath, wondering if I'd done the right thing this afternoon.

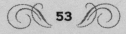

All through today's classes, which had been let out early for YENT testers, I'd thought about contacting Callie. Texting or e-mailing to say good luck. During Ms. Utz's math class, I'd even thought about talking to her before testing to wish her good luck.

But I hadn't. I'd been too worried that approaching her might make her upset and throw her off her game before testing. I didn't want to take any chance at ruining this for her. I was sure some of her friends from Orchard and the stable had been there to give her a pep talk before her ride. Looking down at her and the way she handled Jack, it looked as if I'd done the right thing.

The arena's main door opened and Mr. Conner ushered Mr. Nicholson and two other scouts inside. They took seats along the arena wall, clipboards in hand, prepared to watch the three advanced riders. The dressage markers were in place and the arena was raked clean and smooth aside from the hoof prints where the girls had been warming up.

"Callie's definitely got the edge in dressage," I whispered to Brit. "You've seen her. She's amazing."

Brit nodded. "She's so precise. I learn something every time I watch her."

Mr. Conner motioned for Callie, Julia, and Alison to

come to him in the center of the arena. The three girls rode their horses toward him, stopping them in a line before him.

I gripped the sides of my chair. It was time.

"Julia, Callie, Alison," Mr. Conner said. "Thank you all for coming. Please give a nod to the Youth Equestrian National Team Scouts who have traveled here today to watch you ride."

The girls dipped their heads and the scouts reciprocated.

Mr. Conner turned his head toward the skybox. "And to those of you watching, I am pleased to see you here. I ask that you remain silent during testing."

Mr. Conner smiled at the riders, probably trying to get them to relax. "By random drawing, the order for dressage has been selected. Alison, you're up first. Followed by Callie and then Julia."

The three girls nodded.

"Not good for Julia," Heather whispered to Brit and me. "She's only going to get more nervous."

"I hope not," I said. Julia wasn't my favorite person, but I knew what testing felt like. The stress level was *insane* and it wasn't fun to go last and have to watch the competition before you. Unless they tanked.

"It could go to her advantage if Callie and Alison don't ride well, though," Brit said.

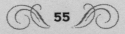

It was almost as if she read my mind.

Heather shot her a look. "And do you *really* think the odds of that are high?"

Brit pressed her Too Faced glossed lips together. She knew Heather was right. We both did.

Callie and Julia rode off to the side of the arena, stopping Jack and Trix to face the arena.

The girls had memorized their tests before today—I'd seen them practicing—so Mr. Conner wouldn't be calling out instructions. It would score them extra points with the judges for memorizing the tests.

Alison rode into the arena at a working trot, halted, and saluted the judges. I took a deep breath. Even though my start at Canterwood had been rocky with Alison, I didn't want her to mess up. She'd been the first of the Trio to make an effort to be friendly toward me.

Sunstruck's pale ears flicked back and forth—he was nervous. Alison knew him well enough to know he needed an extra second before they started. Instead of starting immediately, she waited, letting him settle. It made me feel that she was less nervous if she took her time instead of feeling pressured to start right away because the judges were watching.

After a few more seconds, Alison urged Sunstruck

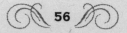

back into an extended trot and his long legs carried him across the arena. His espresso-colored saddle and bridle gleamed. Alison must have spent hours cleaning his tack and it made them look like a more professional pair, if that was even possible. Alison's attire was flawless and her crisp white shirt made her look like the perfect YENT candidate.

She guided Sunstruck toward the next marker and they switched to a working trot. Alison's posture was relaxed as she turned Sunstruck into a twenty meter circle. His curved body was beautiful to watch. He looked looser than he ever had over the past few weeks—a direct result of the hours Alison had worked with him.

As I watched Alison, I thought back over the past couple of weeks of practicing that she and Julia had done. Heather had offered to help both girls, but Alison had been the only one to say yes. Julia had acted as if her own practice sessions were some big secret. She'd ridden by herself most of the time and had spent looong hours in the indoor and outdoor arenas. It was weird that she'd been so unwilling to ride with Alison, especially since they'd always been inseparable.

But the YENT changed people.

Alison eased Sunstruck out of the circle and they made

a smooth transition into a working canter. The gelding seemed to have gotten over his nerves and he was listening to every cue Alison gave him, but still looked fresh and not robotic as if he'd done the routine a zillion times.

I wondered if Julia's routine would look like the last one she'd done late yesterday evening. Trix had seemed bored with the movements—likely from over practicing. She and Heather had gotten into arguments about it when Heather had tried to remind her about the difference between working hard and working too much. I'd excused myself from the arena when Julia had snapped at Heather.

That was something you didn't do unless you wanted to be tortured by the Canterwood Queen. Charm and I had been halfway down the aisle before red-faced Heather had responded.

I shuddered, my attention back on Alison, because I couldn't even imagine the verbal smackdown Heather had given Julia.

Alison finished a couple more circles, only slightly off on one, and headed at a trot back to the center of the arena down the center line. She slowed Sunstruck to a free walk and he seemed to sense they were almost done. An extra spring made him almost bouncy. Alison halted him at X, saluted, and the test was over.

Heather, Brit, and I looked at each other.

"Amazing!" I whispered.

"She deserved that ride," Heather said.

Brit nodded, looking back and forth from us to Alison and Sunstruck. "They both looked great. I'm really happy for her. She deserves a great score for that test."

I looked back at Mr. Robb and he was half out of his chair as if he wanted to clap and cheer for Alison but knew he couldn't. The smile on his face said everything— he couldn't have looked more proud of his daughter. His smile made lines around his eyes crinkle. And even though all three girls were competitors, Mr. and Mrs. Harper and Julia's parents all turned to Mr. Robb and whispered congratulations to him on Alison's ride.

Alison joined Julia at the sidelines with the biggest smile on her face I'd ever seen. Callie held up her palm and the girls did a quiet high five. Alison, still grinning, looked at Julia. But Julia looked *way* less than thrilled. She gave Alison a tight half smile, then stared straight ahead. Alison's smile disappeared and even from the skybox, I could see her shrink down in the saddle.

Brit and I looked at each other.

"Whoa," Brit mouthed.

I shook my head.

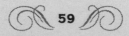

Unbelievable. Yeah, it was Julia and YENT testing was superstressful, but Alison was her friend. Julia had just treated her like a competitor. That's when riding stopped being fun.

Mr. Conner motioned to Callie, signaling her to start whenever she was ready. Callie didn't need another minute to collect herself—she was ready this time. I could tell by the look on her face. When she stopped in the center of the arena and saluted, I knew her ride was going to be amazing.

And I wasn't wrong.

The test seemed to be over in seconds. Callie and Jack hadn't missed a step. When Callie was this focused, there was no stopping her. Even though we weren't best friends anymore, I still wished I could tell her what I thought of her ride. But I was still afraid of throwing her off when she still had two more rounds of testing.

Callie, patting Jack's neck, rode him over to Julia and Alison. Alison smiled at her and both girls were visibly relaxed now that one test was over. I'd wanted to see them both ride, but the test I'd been waiting for was seconds away.

Julia's.

Brit, Heather, and I were silent—not taking our eyes

off Julia. She had the reins tight in her hands and Trix's neck was bowed from the pressure. Even though the bay mare had been stationary while Alison and Julia had tested, her bay chest had darkened from sweat. She'd been calm until Julia had become more and more tense.

Julia put the reins in her left hand, giving Trix a little reprieve, and brushed at her jacket and breeches as if she was swatting away a bug.

If she didn't calm down, this was *not* going to go well.

Mr. Conner waited for Mr. Nicholson and the other scouts to finish scribbling notes about Callie and Jack before he motioned Julia forward.

Julia, not wasting a second, asked Trix to move forward. The mare jumped as if she'd been stung by a bee and trotted quickly to X. Julia halted, did a fast salute to the scouts and Mr. Conner, then started her round.

Her posture toward the first marker was stiff and she kept Trix on an unnecessarily tight rein. Trix's movements to the first marker were tense—probably in response to the pressure from Julia. Glancing over, I caught Heather rubbing her right temple. Julia had to loosen up. Like, right NOW.

Trix and Julia moved to the next marker and, almost as if she'd heard my thoughts through ESP, Julia's body

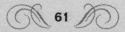

started to relax. Her shoulders dropped, she loosed her legs from the grip they'd had on Trix's sides, and she seemed to breathe again. In return, Trix responded and began to move like the well-trained horse she was.

Heather let out a not-so-quiet breath. *This* was the type of ride Julia needed. The type of ride that could get her onto the YENT. Brit, Heather, and I watched from our spot in the skybox as Julia and Trix kept up the beautiful steps from marker to marker.

Minutes later, a very different Julia and a calm Trix rode down the center of the arena, came to a smooth stop and Julia saluted.

She rode back to Alison and Callie on the side of the arena, easing Trix beside Sunstruck. Callie and Alison both smiled at Julia—not being influenced by the way she'd acted before her ride. Julia smiled, but there was still a narrowed look in her eyes. I wondered if she was unhappy about some part of her ride or if she was thinking that show jumping and cross-country were still left.

Mr. Conner stepped back into the center of the arena.

"Thank you all for your hard work," he said. "I appreciate your effort. You all have the next half hour to yourselves before you need to head to the outdoor arena. We'll start the show jumping round then."

The girls nodded once, then dismounted at Mr. Conner's gesture. Single file, they led their horses out of the arena.

The parents left the skybox, eager to get to their daughters. Heather, Brit, and I waited, letting them out first.

It was *so* time to break down what we'd just seen.

"Julia kept Trix at even pace," Brit said. "But I'm worried about her bad start. I don't know if the scouts will look past that or not."

Heather nodded, squeezing her eyes shut. "I know. I wished she would have been able to relax."

"She did, though," I said. "Maybe the scouts will look past it as nerves because the test had just started."

They'd definitely done that with me. My rides hadn't been even close to perfect, but Mr. Nicholson had taken what he'd called my "potential" into account when he'd made the final decision.

"Maybe." Heather half-nodded. "But compared to Alison's test?"

I'd never seen Heather look so proud before. She acted icy a lot of the time, but when it counted, how much she cared for her friends showed. Now was one of those times.

"Alison made Sunstruck look as if he wasn't even working hard," I added. "Every cue she gave him was seamless."

"Agreed," Heather said. "The only time they were in trouble was when she did a collected trot instead of a free walk during the middle of the test."

We looked at each other—everyone waiting to see if the other would talk about Callie first.

"Callie's ride was strong," I said, taking a breath and deciding to be the first to go.

Brit and Heather nodded.

"She was great," Brit said. "She looked as if she and Jack moved as one—you couldn't separate them."

"Overall, everyone had excellent rides," I said. "I'd never be able to be a scout after being on this side of things. We all know the work and stress that goes into being a YENT rider. It would be hard to judge someone."

"You're deciding their fate as a rider," Brit said. "I wouldn't be able to do that either."

"I would." Heather said, grinning.

We laughed.

"Of course *you* would," I said, fake-rolling my eyes. "Judging people is your second fave thing after riding."

Heather shrugged, looking innocent. "It's actually my *third* favorite. Get it right, Silver."

Heather stepped past us, weaving around the chairs, and headed out of the skybox.

"What's second, then?" Brit asked as we followed Heather out.

Heather turned back to look at us, her mouth open to say something. She closed it, blushing, and sped up going down the stairs.

Heather didn't have to say what was second. I already knew.

Troy.

7

WITH FIRE

AFTER THE SHOW JUMPING ROUND, THE mistakes Julia had made during dressage were almost out of my mind. She'd had the best ride, easily, out of everyone. Callie and Alison hadn't made any mistakes or knocked any jumps, but they hadn't had that . . . *sparkle* Julia had shown. She'd taken all twelve of the jumps, including a tricky triple combination, with fire. It had been as though every second in the arena that Julia had spent with Mr. Conner had gone into her jumping.

She left the arena with a huge smile on her face.

But so had Alison and Callie.

I shifted on the bleachers, turning to look at Heather.

"I have no idea," she said. "Julia could have just wiped out her mistakes from dressage."

Brit zipped up her navy and sky blue PINK hoodie. A chill had started to settle in the air. "Honestly, I wasn't even thinking about scoring when I watched them. All of their rides were so tight and well-paced that I was seriously taking mental notes about what I could do better."

I checked the time on my phone. Four-thirty. Now, time was just going to be suuuper slow while Callie, Julia, and Alison did cross-country. The course was short, to keep the horses and riders from getting exhausted. The girls had walked the course after another break and they'd had a diagram of the jumps to study for over a week.

Since none of us were allowed on course, we had to wait along with everyone else on the crowded metal bleachers to see how each rider did. And that meant also . . . counting the seconds until my date with Jacob.

"Can I see the course diagram?" Brit asked Heather.

"Sure."

They bent over the paper and, as they started to talk, I stopped hearing them and my mind went to tonight. I had no idea what Jacob had planned. The Sweet Shoppe? A movie? A cozy dinner in the common room?

Just thinking about tonight made me feel warm against the fall chill. A date, a real date, with Jacob was something I couldn't even begin to digest. I'd been on dates, obviously, with Eric, but this was my *first* date with Jacob. The boy I'd chatted with at Ms. Utz's office when I'd been a scared newbie, trying to figure out my schedule and what my life was going to be like at Canterwood. The guy I'd spent hours with, playing Mario Kart and bonding over movies during Mr. Ramirez's film class.

Giggling next to me yanked me out of my daydream. I looked at Brit and Heather. They were staring at me with silly grins on their faces.

"What?" I asked. "Why are you looking at me like that?"

"Oooh, I don't know," Brit said in a singsong voice. "I've just never seen you blush over cross-country."

Heather batted her eyelashes, tossing her blond hair in a teasing way. "Silver's thinking about Jaaay-cob."

I couldn't help but laugh. "Okay, okay! I spaced for a second and it's my first date ever with Jacob and I've been waiting forever for him to ask me and—"

"Omigod, take a breath before you hyperventilate," Heather said, shaking her head. "You're *ridiculous*." But she said it with a smile. She knew what this date meant to me and how important it was, especially after all she'd done in the past to get between us.

I listened to Heather, took a deep breath, and focused

my gaze on the course diagram. The riding order had been determined—Julia, Alison, then Callie.

Brit, Heather, and I had eaten lunch with Julia and Alison. Both girls had seemed calm, but excited to start cross-country. It would be the final step of testing and it was the perfect way to let the horses de-stress. Trix and Sunstruck loved cross-country and the course looked liked so much fun—it was a diagram I wanted to save and try sometime.

The course consisted of several hedges, a log jump, a brief trek through part of the creek, and then cantering up and down a few hills to test stamina.

My phone buzzed and I looked at my texts.

Hey Sash—I can't wait to see you tonight! Meet me in the court-yard at 7, okay?

Jacob.

I couldn't type back fast enough.

I'm so excited about tonite. I'll be there @ 7. ☺

"Julia should be coming in any second," Heather said, looking at her phone while I put mine away.

Julia and Trix had done a beautiful turn out of the sky-box and had set off at a strong canter toward the woods.

"There she is," Brit said, pointing to the finish line.

Julia's red protective vest made it easy to spot her. She

let Trix into an easy gallop as she rode between two plastic poles that signaled the end of the course.

A beaming Julia rode Trix up to the bleachers, swinging a leg over the saddle. Ben, already on the ground, grabbed her before her boots touched the grass and hugged her. They'd been BF/GF for awhile and made a cute couple.

"You're done!" Ben said, his pale skin flushed with excitement. "How did it go?"

"It was amazing," Julia said. She loosened Trix's girth, letting the mare breathe. Trix was tired after a long day of testing. Her coat was slick with sweat despite the cool weather, her nostrils flared pink, and her breathing was fast.

Julia's parents stepped down to hug her and pat Trix.

"We're so proud, sweetie," Mr. Myer told her.

"You've got to be exhausted," Mrs. Myer said, brushing back sweaty strands of hair that had escaped from Julia's ponytail. "What do you have left to do?"

Julia hugged Trix's neck. "I've got to have her vitals checked, then Mike or Doug will groom and feed her. They already offered."

"We'll be at The Sweet Shoppe," Mr. Myer said. "Your mom and I are going to grab coffee. When you're ready, come meet us for a bit."

Julia nodded, giving her parents a one-armed hug while she held Trix's reins with the other hand. "The Sweet Shoppe is exactly where I want to be. I'm dying for a *giant* Coke and strawberry cheesecake."

I was surprised that Julia wanted to go to The Sweet Shoppe and not stay to hear how Callie and Alison did. She was full of confidence today.

She turned to Ben. "Want to come?"

Ben nodded. "As if I'd miss celebrating this with you. Text me when you're heading over and I'll be there. I know you made it, Jules."

Julia gave Ben a quick kiss. "Thank you. I'll text you soon."

She turned to us, a satisfied smile on her face. She looked sure, so sure, that her name would be added to the YENT roster tomorrow.

With that, Julia led Trix toward the stable and Alison walked Sunstruck to the starting box. She had to take her time easing the gelding out of the box or he'd leave early and start off at a too-fast gallop. Heather, Brit, and I, along with parents, the scouts, and many of the interme-diate and beginner riders watched as Alison settled herself into the saddle, waiting for the starting signal.

The bell sounded and Alison, keeping a tight rein on

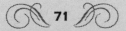

Sunstruck, forced him to turn slowly and do a slow canter. Sunstruck jumped forward a few strides, trying to pull the reins through Alison's gloved fingers. But she didn't let him get away with it. She held him back and, by the time they reached the woods, Sunstruck had settled into the collected canter.

"Good start," Brit said. "If she'd let him gallop when they were supposed to be cantering, she could have gotten him too excited for the course."

"Alison's great about that," Heather said. "She may be quiet, but she knows how to handle him better than anyone I've seen."

While Alison finished her ride, Heather, Brit, and I chatted about the latest stable gossip.

"Did you hear that Lexington's owners are selling him?" Heather asked.

Lexington was a gorgeous steely gray that Mr. Conner had been training.

"Wow," I said. "I wonder if a Canterwood student will buy him."

And we, well, mostly Heather, kept chatting about what was going on around the stable.

"I *did* hear that Andy, Troy, Ben, and a few of the other guys from the team had taken a trail ride a few days ago,"

Brit put in. "Apparently, they found a new trail that's really great for stamina building."

Heather and I looked at each other.

"*So* finding out where that is," I said. Charm and I definitely needed a new course to try.

The time Alison was riding passed faster than I imagined it would. It seemed as if she'd just started when we heard hoofbeats approaching.

Alison came back smiling and went straight for Mr. Robb. As she rode closer to him, he took photos of her grinning at the camera. When Alison reached him, she leaned down to hug him before dismounting.

Heather, Julia, and I surrounded her. She took off her helmet, shaking out her ponytail.

"Omigod, that was so much fun!" she said. "I swear, I totally forgot there were scouts on the course."

"That's great!" Heather said, hugging her friend. "I'm so proud of you."

My head turned toward Heather so fast, it almost gave me whiplash. I'd *never* heard her say something that nice.

To anyone.

Ever.

Apparently, Alison hadn't either. She hugged Heather again, teary. "Thanks," she said.

Heather extracted herself from Alison's arms, shaking her head. "Geez, Alison. Don't turn this into a TV talk show moment."

Heather sounded annoyed, but Alison and I knew her too well. She'd meant every word of what she'd said to Alison.

"Don't worry," Alison said, still giddy from her ride. "I won't tell anyone that you were just supernice to me."

With a smile, she led Sunstruck in for the vet check, and Callie, who'd been trotting Jack in serpentines and circles to loosen him up, headed for the start box at the sign from Mr. Conner.

This time, Heather, Brit, and I sat without saying a word. There was no need for words when Callie rode through the finish line and headed for her parents. The smile on her face said it all—she'd done well.

Extremely well.

8

LUCKY NUMBER SEVEN

AFTER THE TESTING, BRIT AND I HEADED BACK to our room with no clear idea who might have made the YENT.

"At least we'll know tomorrow," Brit said. "The wait feels long to us and we're not even the ones testing."

"I totally remember how that felt," I said, grabbing what I needed for the shower. I wanted to have *plenty* of time to get ready for my date with Jacob. I hadn't decided what I was going to wear yet, but Brit had gladly agreed to help. "I couldn't sleep most of the night and I was shaking before we to see Mr. Nicholson."

"Me too. It was such a big deal. I really hope that no matter what happens tomorrow, who ever doesn't make it, that it doesn't destroy the Trio. They're all friends and I hope they're all able to remember that."

I headed for the bathroom. "I hope so too. But if Alison makes it and Julia doesn't or vice versa, I really don't know how."

The one person I worried about most was Julia. She was already teetering on the edge and I worried that even Alison and Heather couldn't put her back together if everything fell apart for her.

Brit settled onto her bed, pulling out and flipping through the Pottery Barn Teen catalog while I jumped in the shower. I'd bought a pair of pink exfoliating gloves last week and I squeezed half a handful (waaay too much!) shower gel onto the gloves. I was covered in bubbles that ran down to my feet. I scrubbed my skin until it was pink and soft. I took extra time rinsing my hair to get out any scent of the stable. Then, I grabbed the bottle of Bumble and bumble Creme de Coco shampoo that I shared with Brit and lathered up my hair until it was covered in bubbles.

I took my time in the bathroom, spraying on leave-in conditioner before slathering my body in thick lotion. After my hair was blown dry, I flatironed it and ended with a finishing spray to keep my hair shiny and soft.

Wrapping my body in a chocolate brown towel, I

stepped out of the bathroom and headed for my closet.

Brit, lying on her stomach, was on her laptop. "Your phone buzzed a bunch of times while you were in the shower," she said.

I picked up my phone. There were six new "add as a friend" notifications from FaceSpace.

"Weird," I said. "A bunch of people from some of my classes wanted to add me as a friend on FaceSpace. I've only talked to them, like, a few times. Ever."

"Who are they?" Brit asked. I handed her my phone and she looked at the names. "I'm friends with all of them. You should totes add them."

She typed something into her laptop, then looked up at me. "If you add six more people, you'll have two more friends than Heather."

"What? No way."

"Way."

Brit showed me Heather's profile and then mine. She was right.

That was *beyond* weird. I couldn't help but think it had to be some kind of mistake.

"FaceSpace's counter must be wrong," I said.

"It's not wrong, silly," Brit said. "Go get ready!"

Brit opened her own profile, starting to update her

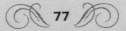

status. I looked at her friend count. She had more friends than Heather *and* me.

Combined.

I put down my phone, starting back to my closet. "But why are they friending *me* all of a sudden? And six in, what? Half an hour?"

Brit looked up from her screen. "You're more popular than you think. Of course people want to be your friend."

I still didn't get it—my social status at school hadn't changed, except for my friendship with Heather,—but I didn't have time to think about it. And anyway, I didn't care if I had two friends or twenty. In half an hour, I had to meet Jacob in the courtyard.

"What should I wear?" I asked Brit. "I've got two ideas, but they might not be any good."

I rifled through my closet, gathered the clothes, and laid them on my bed.

"Hmmm, let's see." Brit got off her bed and stood in front of my clothes, looking at what I'd selected.

One outfit was a ribbed V-neck heather gray sweater, a deep-plum-colored A-line skirt, opaque black tights, and ankle boots. Sophisticated, yet girly with the pretty skirt.

The other option was a three-quarters sleeve pink shirt, a black cardigan, a black ruffle skirt, and knee-high boots.

"What about a switch up?" Brit asked. "I love what you chose, but think about this . . ."

She picked up the heather gray sweater and plum-colored skirt with the boots.

"Gray and purple are the new black for fall," Brit said. "I haven't seen anyone around campus wearing that pairing of colors yet, so you'll look amazing *and* be a trendsetter."

"I love it!" I said. "That's such a great outfit." And I definitely was NOT a trendsetter on campus, but if Brit and I were happy with the clothes—and they seemed as if Jacob would like them—that's all that mattered.

I slipped into the clothes while Brit finished homework. In front of our full-length mirror, I studied the outfit we'd assembled.

"This *really* does look okay, right?" I asked. "I know I'm being a total freak about this—I've been on dates before. But . . ."

"But this is *Jacob*," Brit finished.

I grabbed my makeup case and sat on my desk chair. "Yeah, it *is* Jacob."

I didn't have to say anything else—I'd already explained our history to Brit. She knew how I felt about this date. It was something I'd been wanting, something I'd been dreaming about for a long time.

"You look great, Sasha," Brit said. "I promise. Friends don't let friends commit crimes of fashion."

Giggling, I reached into my makeup bag and pulled out concealer. And the entire time I got ready, Brit distracted me with gossip she'd heard around campus and a story about one of her dates gone wrong.

When she finished telling me, I was laughing so hard that I couldn't even apply a coat of mascara. The wand was wobbling too much in my shaking hand.

"So," I said, trying to breathe and not ruin my eyeliner with tears. "The guy knocked over a giant tub of extra buttery popcorn in your lap at the movie theater?"

Brit nodded with a pretend-grim face. "Yep. And when he freaked out and leaned over to try to help me pick up the pieces, he knocked over his Sprite. All. Over. Me."

"Oh, nooo way! That's awful!" I said. Finally able to control my laughter, I applied a light coat of brown-black mascara and looked through my lip gloss collection.

Brit, knowing how serious choosing a lip gloss was to me, was silent while I held up different tubes and looked at them.

"This one," I said, after a few more seconds.

I showed the Sephora Nectar Shine in apricot to Brit.

"That looks perfect," she said. "It'll be semi-sheer

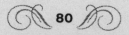

with just a hint of peachy color. That'll look great with your subtle smoky eyes. Not too overpowering."

"Thanks, Brit. That was exactly the look I was going for."

I applied the gloss, zipped up my boots, and grabbed my purse and phone. A pair of simple silver hoops seemed like a nice touch with my charm bracelet. It had a tiny silver horse that my parents had given me before I'd come to Canterwood. It used to have a heart and horseshoe—gifts from Eric before we'd broken up.

I checked my phone. It was 6:53. Perfect timing.

"My little Sasha is all ready for her date with Jacob," Brit said, giving me a teasing smile.

"I think I'm ready. I'm so nervous, but I don't know why! It's Jacob."

Brit got up, putting a hand on my elbow. "I'm sure he's nervous too. He wants to impress you and make everything perfect. You're going to be fine—I swear. You've been waiting for this for a long time. Decide to just have fun and your nerves will disappear."

Brit reached over and held up her phone. "And if he dumps popcorn on you or spills Sprite on your lap and you need to bolt, BBM me, and I'll call you with an emergency."

I hugged her. "You're the best."

Taking my fiftieth deep breath of the night, I gave Brit a tiny wave and left our room. I looked at the text from Jacob again and when I read the words, it made the nervousness I felt in my stomach go away.

Can't wait 2 c u @ 7.

I couldn't stop myself from hurrying across campus. Jacob hadn't told me anything about what he'd planned for our date, so I had no idea where we were going after the courtyard.

The September sun had started to set behind me, casting an orange glow over campus. I was glad for my cardigan—the setting sun had started a comfortable chill across the quiet campus. The quiet, though, was odd. Usually, people were always doing *something.* Playing Frisbee, tossing a football, or practicing cheerleader routines on the grounds. But, tonight, lights shone from the dorm rooms and I only spotted a few students in the distance leaving the science building.

My boots clicked against the cobblestone part of the courtyard. And, as I waked toward the center, I saw him.

Jacob, standing in front of the fountain, turned, and just as he did, the old-fashioned street-lights started to flicker on. If it had been a movie scene, I would have said it was sooo not real.

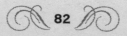

But it was. And then I noticed what I'd missed because my attention had been focused on Jacob—candles.

Everywhere. He'd placed cream-colored pillar candles all around the fountain and the flames reflected the almost-silent water that streamed down a granite stone, refreshing the water for the koi that I loved to watch every time I walked by.

He walked toward me, his lightly tanned athletic face tilted in a smile. He'd put on a green polo shirt—a color I loved on him—and black pants.

"Hi," I said.

"Hi," he said, reaching to take my right hand. "You look gorgeous, Sasha."

"Thank you. Brit helped me pick out the clothes. I wanted to look . . . well, okay on our first date."

Jacob's eyes were intense on mine. "You look *so* much better than okay."

I blushed, hoping the faint lighting would help hide the pinkness in my cheeks. "So do you," I said.

"Come with me."

Jacob, holding my hand, led me toward the stone bench across from the fountain. We both sat down, facing each other.

"The candles look so beautiful," I said. "How did you

manage to convince Headmistress Drake to let you light them here?"

"Oh, I just told her that I was taking a very special girl on our first date and I knew how much she loved candles."

I smiled. "That was way easier than I thought."

Jacob laughed. "Welll, what you *don't* see is the mini–fire extinguisher she made one of the janitors give me. It's on the other side of the fountain."

I laughed, a familiar feeling of comfort starting to come over me.

"I *knew* there had to be a catch."

Jacob laughed with me, then placed his other hand on top of the one he was holding. "Do you know why I asked you to meet me here?"

I didn't have to think about it for a second. "Of course I do. This is where we met after fall break. We decided to try dating when we were here together. I'm so glad you brought me here."

Jacob smiled. "I'm really glad to hear you say that, Sash, because we're going to be here for a while."

I looked at him, curious. "What do you mean?"

Jacob gestured toward the fountain. "I thought we'd do something a little different—something away from everyone else."

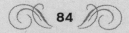

I loved the sound of that.

"I went to The Slice yesterday," Jacob continued. "I asked them if they'd deliver to a sort of unusual place."

"Here?" I almost bounced on the bench.

"Right here. They said yes and any minute now, a half-cheese and half-pepperoni pizza will be here for us."

"Jacob, that was such a great idea! This is so special."

Jacob looked at me with a soft gaze. "You're special, Sash. I kept going back and forth in my brain trying to think if this was a good idea or a cheesy one. But then I thought about how important that moment was to me— when you said you wanted to try being together—and then I knew it was the right choice."

"It was *definitely* the right choice," I said, my voice soft. "I wouldn't have wanted our first date to be anywhere else."

At the same moment, Jacob and I leaned close to each other and our lips touched. Our lips were warm against each other's and I almost forgot where I was. We leaned back, our faces still close.

We smiled at each other and I wanted to capture every second of this moment.

It was perfect.

We stayed like that for a few more seconds, then Jacob put an arm around my shoulders. It felt so good to be near

him—I was happy no matter what we were doing.

"How are things in Orchard?" Jacob asked. "Leaving Winchester and not being Paige's roommate anymore had to be major for you."

I hadn't really talked about it too much with anyone except Brit and the Trio.

"Leaving Paige was the hardest thing I've done since I came here," I said. "Even harder than trying out for the YENT." I paused, taking a breath. "But I couldn't stay there. Not in that room. Not with her after what she did. Paige was my best friend and I know, I know—I could have told her about us, but that was different."

Jacob nodded, touching my arm.

"Paige told Callie the truth about us and never told me. And Paige said she did it because I kept my meeting with you in secret and Callie was her friend. But that was *my* secret to tell, not hers."

"I'm so sorry things happened that way," Jacob said. "I really wish I'd been able to tell Callie the truth like we'd planned. When I got that message from you that Callie already knew—I had to read it twice. I almost didn't believe it."

I shook my head. "It wasn't even like Paige at all. I looked at her before I texted Brit about moving in and it

was like I'd never seen Paige before. The best friend part of her was gone. I didn't hesitate about texting Brit."

"I think you made the right choice," Jacob said. "You both need space. I'm sure there's a better chance at repairing your friendship if you're not living together right now."

It took me a minute, but I finally nodded. "It's hard to get over that, but I do miss her. And look at *me*—I've made so many mistakes too. But I need a little time."

"Absolutely," Jacob said. "It'll give you a clearer perspective on the whole thing."

Jacob was one of the best listeners. That was something I'd liked about him from the second we'd met in the guidance counselor's office. He'd listened to me ramble about being a new student and, in a Jacob-way, had made me feel welcome.

Jacob ran his index finger over my knuckles. "Do you like living with Brit?"

"It's so great. It's like we've known each other forever—I've never made friends with someone so fast, not even Callie or Paige."

"That's great. It would have been so hard on you if you'd moved into Orchard and you and Brit had found out you weren't good roommates."

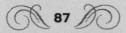

"I know. It's strange, though. I was never worried about that with her. If things hadn't happened the way they did with Paige, I probably would have tried to get a triple to see if we could all live together next semester."

"And things seemed to have really calmed down with you and the Trio," Jacob said, shifting on the bench.

"They definitely have. I mean, aside from Julia still barely tolerating me, Heather and Alison are friends now. It's just . . . odd how things have shifted."

Jacob smiled. "They all, especially Heather, used to hardcore go after you and now you're all friends. It's pretty cool of you to let go of the past and be their friend. Not many people could do that."

His compliment made me blush for the second time. *Omigod*, I yelled at myself. *Stop it!*

"Thanks for saying that, but it really was a shift between all of us," I said. "We kind of all grew up, I guess. It's easier for us to get along than to hate each other. It was exhausting!" I looked down and realized that I was rubbing my thumb over the top of his hand. And I didn't feel embarrassed or awkward. I hadn't even realized that it had gotten dark and that a giant full moon had started to rise.

We both looked up, kind of startled, when a high

schooler stopped in front of us, pizza box and two cans of Diet Coke in hand.

Jacob stood, taking his wallet out of his back pocket. "Thanks," he said to the pizza guy as he swapped the pizza and soda for money.

The pizza guy left and Jacob reached beside the bench and pulled out a Boston Red Sox bag.

"Come with me," he said.

I followed him behind the bench, to the grass. We stopped under a streetlight and Jacob put the bag down and sodas down.

"Can you hold the pizza for a sec?" he asked.

"Sure." I took the box and watched as he pulled a gray blanket from the bag, spreading it on the grass. He took out two plates, a handful of napkins and set two places for us.

"Jacob," I said. "This is so perfect! I would have been happy to have eaten on the bench. This really is amazing."

"I thought a picnic would be fun." Jacob took the pizza box from me, his fingers brushing against mine. "A little quieter than eating at The Slice."

We settled down on the blanket and Jacob served me a slice of pepperoni pizza.

"This is so good. Thank you."

Jacob smiled. "I'm glad you like everything, Sash."

"I do. And, seriously, we talked about me and all of my stuff. What's new with you? How's football?"

Jacob and I talked and laughed until the moonlight cast pale shadows over both of us. This was the most unforgettable first date I would ever have. I was sure of it.

9

IT'S ALL UP TO HIM

ALL DAY THURSDAY, JULIA WALKED AROUND with a *look* on her face—a smugness. A look of assured victory. In the hallway before math, I saw Heather and hurried toward her.

"What's going on with Julia?" I asked. "I've seen her a few times today and she looks as if she already knows. Like Mr. Nicholson told her she made the YENT."

Heather shifted her armload of books, sighing. "It's *all* she would talk about last night. Alison fell asleep early because she was exhausted from the day, but Julia was sooo hyper. She did well at tryouts, we know that. But she didn't make the team for sure."

"But you can't tell her that," I said. "It'll hurt her feelings."

A look passed over Heather's face. "I didn't say anything last night and it's almost time for announcements anyway. But she's going to *lose* it if she doesn't make it. She's always been confident about her riding, but I don't know why she's being so cocky about this."

The bell rang and we stared at each other before Heather shrugged.

"We just have to wait and see," she said. "There's nothing we can do about Julia. It's all up to Mr. Nicholson now."

"See you at the stable," I said.

We split up and headed for our classes. I sat down in Ms. Utz's math class and opened my notebook.

I wrote my name and date on a clean sheet of paper, then started doodling in the margins.

"See her charm bracelet? I heard that Sasha's ex-boyfriend from Union got it for her."

I kept my eyes on my paper, pretending to draw but listening to the whispering behind me.

"She's had, like, six boyfriends and they all gave her charms," the girl continued. "But she took them off when she broke up with them."

"The horse charm is so cute," another girl whispered. "And I don't even like horses."

"I told my parents I wanted a bracelet just like that for my birthday," the first girl said.

"My dad said I could get one if my grades were good at the end of the semester," said the other girl.

I sat there, stunned. I'd *never* heard anything like this about me! No one had ever wanted anything I owned. Everyone in our grade always looked to Heather, Julia, and Alison for fashion, jewelry, and style direction. *Definitely* not me.

"Hey," Brit said, sliding into the seat next to me.

"Omigod, get out your phone!" I whispered. There was no way I wanted the girls behind us to hear me talking about them.

Brit pulled out her BlackBerry and I opened BlackBerry Messenger.

Sasha Silver:

U won't believe this

Brit Chan:

What? What? Tell me!! O_O

Sasha Silver:

2 girls behind us were talking about me. Well, my bracelet.

Brit Chan:

What abt it? Did they say something mean abt it? :/

Sasha Silver:

No—they actually asked their parents 4 one exactly like it! :S

Brit Chan:

Cool!!! ☺ It IS v pretty. U should be flattered, S.

Sasha Silver:

They were talking total rumors 2. Like, how I have charms for all of my ex-boyfriends that I broke up with. Where did THAT come from?!

Brit Chan:

LOLOL. I didn't know a total heartbreaker moved into my room. :D

Sasha Silver:

Ha. Ha. :p It was just weird.

Ms. Utz walked into the room, forcing Brit and me to shove our phones under the desk.

"Hi, class," Ms. Utz said.

Whoa. It almost hurt to look at her outfit. Ms. Utz, a wrestler on the weekends, was over six feet tall. And her shirt choice for the day? A green and yellow plaid shirt with matching green pants. That much plaid looked like an optical illusion.

Sasha Silver:

Ouch abt the shirt, right?!

Brit Chan:

Major. Ouch.

Sasha Silver:

I srsly can't sit thru many more classes. I need YENT results now.

Brit Chan:

I know. What's ur gut feeling?

I moved my phone to the side when Ms. Utz moved behind her desk to take attendance.

Sasha Silver:

Callie. U?

Brit Chan:

I think Alison.

Sasha Silver:

Saw H and Julia a bunch of times today. J rlly seems 2 think she already made it.

Brit Chan:

Eeek. Well, we're gonna find out v v soon.

As Ms. Utz finished taking attendance, Brit and I put away our phones.

Classes finally ended for the day and Brit, Heather, Julia, Alison, and I hurried toward the stable. Mr. Nicholson would be making the announcement in fifteen minutes.

"C'mon, guys," Julia said, walking ahead of us. "We're going to be late if we don't walk faster."

"Jules, chill," Heather said. "Seriously. We're two minutes away."

Julia didn't respond—she stayed two steps in front of us the entire walk from the courtyard where we'd met. We went to Mr. Conner's office and his door was shut. Voices at a low volume were coming from inside. Julia started toward the door, tiptoeing.

"Julia!" Heather hissed. "Sit down." Heather grabbed her friend's arm and yanked her onto the bench outside of Mr. Conner's office.

I looked over at Alison, who hadn't said a word since we'd met up. She gave me a shaky smile. "This part sucks," she said.

"I know," I said.

And I remembered the waiting. Each second had felt like an hour.

"Mr. Conner will call you in any second," I said, trying to make Alison feel better. She was getting paler by the second.

The four of us looked up when Callie walked into the hallway. She sat at the bench across from us, glancing at each of us for a second. She didn't look nervous—she looked focused like always. Calm and ready to hear the results, whatever they were.

I had to wish her good luck. I just had to. Just as I started to open my mouth, the door to Mr. Conner's office opened.

He didn't seem surprised to see Heather, Brit, and I there waiting with Callie, Julia, and Alison.

"Hello, everyone," Mr. Conner said.

"Hi, Mr. Conner," we said back.

"Mr. Nicholson is waiting in my office," Mr. Conner said. "Unlike last time, he's going to have the three of you come in at the same time. He wants to make this as fast and painless as possible."

They were sooo lucky. Last time, Mr. Nicholson had called us in one by one. The wait had been excruciating.

"You may come with me into my office," Mr. Conner said. "But before you go, I want to tell each of you who tested that I'm extremely proud to have you riding for my stable. No matter what the outcome, Julia, Alison, and Callie, you all tried your best during testing. There was not one moment when I was disappointed with your performances."

"Thank you," Callie said. Julia and Alison added their thanks. Mr. Conner didn't offer up praise like that too often and when he did, it meant so much. I hoped that it would mean *something* to the girls who didn't make the team.

Mr. Conner gestured for the three girls to stand and follow him.

"Good luck, guys," Heather said.

"You've got this," Brit added.

"Good luck," I said. "You all worked really hard."

The three girls gave us all tight smiles and turned, following Mr. Conner a few steps down the hallway to his office. He let them walk inside first, then shut the door behind him.

Heather, Brit, and I simultaneously leaned back, resting against the wooden wall.

We were quiet for several minutes. Even though I wasn't waiting to find out my YENT fate, the waiting seemed to drag on just as long.

"Whoever makes it will be a good addition to the team," Heather said. Her tone, though soft, seemed to echo through the hallway.

"Definitely," Brit said. "Each of them worked so hard to get here. I'm so nervous, it feels like *I'm* the one waiting for my decision."

"Me too," I said.

We lapsed into silence.

When Mr. Conner's door finally opened, we all jumped. I stood and so did Brit and Heather.

The three girls walked out of the office and my eyes flicked to each of their faces. I saw Callie first and I knew.

Callie was on the YENT.

She wasn't grinning or gloating, but there was a look of relief and quiet happiness.

"Congratulations, Callie," I said. All along, I knew she'd make it. Callie deserved it. She should have made it the first time she'd tried out. But she was on the team now and that meant we'd have to find a way to coexist.

"Thank you," she said.

Alison looked as if she was going to burst into tears at any second, but she walked over and managed a wavery smile. Everyone else chimed in with their congratulations to Callie. Everyone except for Julia.

Callie, ever the professional, turned to Julia and Alison. "I'm sorry you didn't make it," she said. "It could have been any one of us."

Callie walked down the hallway, leaving the Trio, Brit, and me in the hallway.

"This is *ridiculous!*" Julia whispered, not so quietly. "I worked every single day to make that team. How could Mr. Nicholson pick CALLIE?"

"Julia, shh," I said. "Mr. Conner and Mr. Nicholson will hear you."

"I don't care!" she half-yelled. "Does that even matter now? I didn't make it. I did *everything* and I didn't make it.

After everything, after Jasmine and not being able to test the first time—it's so wrong. I—"

"Let's go before you get in trouble," Alison said, still calm. Her brown eyes were sad, but she was holding it together even when Julia was acting like an insensitive brat.

"Aren't you even a little bit mad?" Julia asked, whipping her head around to glare at Alison. "*You* didn't make it either. Callie did."

"Julia," Heather's voice had a warning tone to it.

But Alison straightened and kept her composure. "I know I didn't make it. And I'm sad and frustrated that I didn't. But no, I'm not mad at myself or Callie or anyone. I tried and I didn't make it."

I just stared at Alison, never feeling more proud of her. She was hurting and dealing with her friend who was completely freaking out.

"Fine," Julia said. "Just be all Alison about it—like everything else. I'm over this."

She stomped away and Heather, Alison, and I looked at each other.

"You okay?" I asked Alison. "I'm sorry that happened after getting news like that."

Alison pulled her long hair over one shoulder. "I'm

sad, obviously. I really, really wanted to be on the YENT. But I *will* try again. I'm not giving up."

Heather gave her a one-armed hug and Alison leaned into her best friend.

"I'm going to talk to Julia," Heather said. She had the tone in her voice that scared me. "What she did was so beneath her and superimmature."

"She's handling it her own way," Alison said. "Don't get into a fight with her over that. It's not worth it. I can handle my own battles."

Heather stared at Alison for a second, then nodded. "I know you can. But she better apologize."

We headed out of the hallway and left the stable. There were no lessons today since Mr. Conner was driving Mr. Nicholson to the airport. I wanted to visit Charm, but Alison, and even Julia, needed moral support right now.

"What do you want to do tonight?" Brit asked Alison. "We should do something fun, right guys?" She looked at Heather and me.

"Definitely," Heather said.

"I'm in," I said.

We skipped the sidewalk, taking a shortcut through the grass to Orchard.

"I'd like that," Alison said, giving us a tiny smile. "I

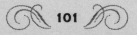

think we should have fun tonight. Maybe a movie and takeout in the common room?"

"Done," Heather said. She playfully elbowed Alison. "I'll even let you pick out the food."

That made Alison laugh. "Wow. I shouldn't make the YENT every day."

Together, we all walked back to the Trio's suite, ready for a night of distraction. Secretly, I was looking forward to it. It had finally sunk in that I'd be practicing with Callie again. I had no idea how we'd work together in the arena at the same time. I didn't have much time to think about it—the first YENT practice with Callie was tomorrow.

10

HEARTS AND KISSES

I WAS SITTING IN HISTORY CLASS WHEN MY
BlackBerry vibrated on my leg.

I looked down and saw a typing sign next to Brit's
name on BlackBerry Messenger.

Brit Chan:

U hear abt it yet?

Sasha Silver:

Hear about what?

Brit Chan:

A Canterwood gossip blog.

Sasha Silver:

??

Brit Chan:

It's anonymous. First post went up an hr ago.

Sasha Silver:

What's it about?

Brit Chan:

Bashing the school & how u have 2 b popular 2 make it @ CC.

Sasha Silver:

Whoa. I want to read it before our lesson.

Brit Chan:

Me 2. Got 2 go, but TTYL.

Sasha Silver:

K. Bye.

I put my phone down and hurried to scribble down the notes I'd missed. An anonymous gossip blogger? It could be anybody—a high schooler, someone in my grade— maybe even someone in my class.

Through the rest of class, I tried to concentrate, but I couldn't. I wanted to read the blog!

After class, I raced back to my dorm. Brit and I reached the door at the same time, laughing. I'd almost gotten tangled in the cotton spider web Halloween decoration that was at the entrance of the hallway because I hadn't been paying attention.

"Good timing," she said.

"No kidding. I practically ran back here so I'd have

enough time to read the post and get dressed before our lesson."

"Me too," Brit said.

We unlocked our door and threw down our backpacks. They'd barely hit the floor when Brit opened her laptop and awakened it from sleep mode.

We both hovered as she typed an address in Firefox— www.canterwoodcrestgossip.com.

A bright purple page with a white text box pulled up. It was a simple blog that looked innocent, but the words were anything but that.

Canterwood Crest

If anyone's paying attention to what's going on at Canterwood Crest "Academy," they might notice a problem. Not a little problem, but an issue that's ridiculously rampant through campus.

Figured it out?

I didn't think so.

I'll spell it out for you. There's a hierarchy on campus. And that order of social status has started to slip.

But that's not going to happen.

New students, recent and past, have shaken up the leaders of each grade, one in particular, and that's something I won't tolerate.

Of course there's no way I'd tell you where I am in the rankings

of things. But just know that I'm watching everything and I'm going to get what I want.

Hearts and kisses

"Whoooa," I said. "Who's writing this? It's crazy!"

Brit, with eyes still on the screen, shook her head. "I don't know. It's offensive to the students *and* the school. This is going to be pulled so fast—I know Canterwood's tech team will figure it out."

"Whoever wrote this is going to be suspended, if not expelled," I said. "If you have to blog about something like this, at least do it on a locked MyJournal or something just to vent."

"There are so many possibilities of people who could be doing it," I added. "It could be anyone."

Brit shut her computer lid, looking at me. "And that's exactly what the blogger wants—for us to wonder."

11

"PROFESSIONAL" DRAMA

I CHECKED OUR PURPLE BEDSIDE CLOCK COVERED in glittery stars. "We better get ready, or we're going to be late."

Brit looked at the clock, jumping off her bed. We pulled riding clothes out of our closet. I slid into my coziest pair of avocado green breeches with comfy suede knees with extra padding. A purple V-neck sweater complemented the green and, stepping back and forth out of each other's way, Brit and I changed and freshened up from a day of classes.

Even though Mr. Conner frowned on us wearing perfume or body spray in class, I spritzed a tiny bit of Burberry Brit perfume (hello, major sale online!) on my wrists. Oddly enough, Charm loved the scent. Maybe it reminded him of me when I was in class all day. When I'd been gone over break, I'd sprayed a tiny bit on his blanket to hopefully comfort him and remind him that I'd be back soon.

I brushed my hair into low ponytail and applied a coat of clear lip gloss.

Brit did her own hair in a beautiful French braid and looked sleek in black breeches, tall boots, and a crew-neck red shirt.

"Ready?" she asked.

"Def," I said.

But I wasn't. I mean, I was dressed and ready to leave, but not so much for the part about spending a lesson with Callie.

Both of us rushed out the door, hurrying for the stable. Since today was the first lesson with Callie, Mr. Conner was easing her into it by starting with only an afternoon lesson. After that, we'd add in morning lessons, too. It would be different to have a roommate who was on the same schedule—one who'd be getting up early with me to ride. That was going to be a huge change in my day-to-day routine.

"Do you think things will be superawkward?" I asked Brit.

"Because of Callie?" she asked.

"Yeah. We haven't ridden together in forever and now she's on the YENT."

We broke into a faster walk, weaving around the other students who were also rushing to sports or extracurricular activities.

"Callie seems like a very professional rider," Brit said, brushing her bangs out of her eyes. "I don't think she's going to be weird or mean to you during lessons."

"I don't think so either," I said. "And Mr. Conner would never allow it. I'm just worried that things will be off and neither of us will be able to concentrate."

Brit and I reached the stable and gathered our horses' tack. "If you stay cool, I'm sure Callie will too," Brit said. "Just act like it's any other lesson and it'll be fine."

"Thanks, B," I said. "See you at the warm up."

We split up and I went straight for the other being who could comfort me the most—Charm.

I walked down the aisle, not seeing Callie, and sighed with relief when I reached Charm's stall.

I slid open the lock, slipping inside. He seemed to sense immediately that I needed him. He walked over from where he'd been standing in the corner and stopped in front of me so I could put my arms around his neck.

"Hi, guy," I said. "I'm sooo nervous about today."

Then I thought about Charm.

"But you're going to be happy. Guess why?"

I let go of Charm and looked in his eyes. He gazed back, seeming to want to know the answer.

"Jack and Callie made the YENT," I told him. "That means you'll get to see Jack every day again. I know you missed him."

Charm, seeming to recognize his old best friend's name, bobbed his head. I rubbed his blaze and stood with him for a few minutes, feeling safe and enjoying the escape from the noise around us.

"Let's get you tacked up," I said at last.

I took Charm by the halter, leading him out of his sawdust-filled stall and into the aisle. There was a free pair of crossties in front of his stall and I clipped them to the side rings of his halter.

"I think you need a supergrooming," I told him.

I took my time brushing his already clean coat, combing his tangle free mane and tail and picking his hooves. It was a stalling technique and I was dangerously close to running late, but I almost didn't care. Part of me was less afraid to face Mr. Conner than to ride in the arena with Callie for the first time. I tacked up Charm, then kept him

standing in the aisle while I pretended to adjust the girth.

"Siiilver, let's go," Heather said as she walked past me and headed for the arena. "We're riding in the outdoor arena. So stop stalling and move before we're late."

I knew she was right. I had to just go and face Callie.

"Coming," I said.

Charm and I lagged behind Heather and Aristocrat as we went down the aisle and toward the outdoor arena.

When I reached the arena, Brit and Heather were warming up their horses. Brit halted Apollo, then worked on backing him in a straight line. Apollo, who always had beautiful lines, tucked his shin and moved straight back, not even hesitating. He was a well-trained horse and I loved watching him move. I wished, more and more, that Brit owned him. Instead, she had been leasing him for the past six months from a girl who was away at college. The lease was for a year and Brit could lose Apollo if the girl decided to take him back. They were a perfect pair—Brit deserved to have Apollo as her own. I didn't even want to think about Brit losing him . . .

Across the arena, Heather was taking Aristocrat through spirals that got tighter and tighter. The chestnut, a few shades darker than Aristocrat, curved his body without the slightest sign of strain. Heather had been working

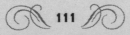

hard to keep him supple by doing lots of lunge work—
something I wanted to do more of with Charm.

I eased Charm into a free walk and let him walk along
the rail. He was in a great mood today—he seemed to
know I needed extra support from him.

Brit turned Apollo around, heading in my direction.

"How're you doing?" she asked.

I settled deep in Charm's saddle, determined to keep
his good mood going. He didn't deserve to be stressed
after such a great start to our warm-up.

"I'm a little on edge," I said. "I don't know how Callie's
going to act toward me, but I'm *sure* she's going to be professional. She'll probably just ignore me."

Brit gave me a half smile. "I'm sorry you're nervous.
But remember—you've got Heather and me in the arena
with you. You're not alone."

"I know—and thanks."

"Want to trot?" Brit asked.

"Definitely," I said.

We squeezed our legs against our horses' sides and
as they started to trot, Callie and Black Jack entered the
arena. Callie had brushed the beautiful gelding to a shining black—his dark coat stark against the white English
saddle pad.

Callie, probably feeling as I had during my first YENT lesson, had put extra effort into dressing up. She wore maroon breeches that I hadn't seen before and a black long sleeve shirt. Charm, seeing Jack, would have paused mid-trot if I didn't encouraged him to keep going. But as we followed Brit and Apollo, leaving Jack and Callie behind, Charm tried to turn his head to see his friend and, for a reason I didn't know, I let him stop.

Jack, strained against the reins, stretching his neck toward Charm.

And Callie let Jack walk over.

Tension rippled through my muscles.. I was *so* over drama—all I wanted to do was focus on the lesson—and I had to hope that the Callie I used to know wanted the same. My fingers gripped the reins and my heart rate sped up, making me all the more happy to have Charm with me.

Callie halted Jack in front of Charm and the two horses sniffed muzzles.

"Hey," I said, my tone cautious, but friendly.

"Hey," Callie echoed.

We both looked down, then back at each other.

"Callie—"

"Sasha—"

We spoke at the same time.

"Go ahead," I said, not wanting her to think I was interrupting and make her angry.

"I just wanted to say that I don't want things to be weird when we practice. Our personal drama has to be separate from this. And I know you know that."

"I do. The YENT is too important to both of us for our issues to follow us into the arena. Plus, it wouldn't be fair to Heather and Brit. We'd be dragging down the team."

Callie reached down to adjust her left stirrup iron. She looked back at me, a calm resolve on her face. Maybe, just maybe, things were going to be okay with us on the same team. I certainly hadn't expected Callie to talk to me on the first day of practice.

"I feel exactly the same way. So, in the arena, we're teammates."

I smiled. This was going waaay better than I'd expected, "Definitely."

"But not friends," Callie said.

She turned Jack away and they moved at a smooth trot down the arena.

I stared after her, almost not able to digest how fast our conversation had gone wrong. I *knew* Callie and I weren't friends, but to hear her say it again, to my face, stung.

A lot.

You can't let this throw you off, I told myself. *You were prepared for this.*

But no matter how much I'd tried to ready myself, it still hurt.

I tapped my boots gently against Charm's sides, asking him to trot. We followed behind Apollo and kept our distance from Callie. I didn't want to get to close to her and have her think I was being "friendly" or anything.

No one said a word while we finished our warm-up. Never a second late, Mr. Conner walked into the arena on time.

"Hi, girls," he said. He turned to Callie. "Welcome to your first official YENT practice. We're all glad to have you here."

Callie smiled. "Thank you. I'm really excited about the team."

Mr. Conner smoothed his shirt. "Before we get started, I wanted to take a brief moment to remind you of our priorities as riders. You're all here to learn about horses—from in-depth care to basic medical training—and yes, you're on this team to become stronger riders. When we begin training for the Huntington Classic, I don't want any of you to forget that. We will *not* be a team that only

focuses on shows. There are many more important aspects to your careers as riders."

Heather, Callie, Brit, and I all nodded. That had been Mr. Conner's message since the day I'd started at Canterwood—he'd never wanted us to become riders who didn't muck our horses' stalls, didn't care about our horses' health, or obsessed over competition alone.

And each of us had been too focused on showing before. I'd moved past that phase—I'd realized the hard way that if, like Mr. Conner said, I wanted this to be my career, I couldn't make competing my entire life. Once I'd made that choice and had started to find the balance with school, boys, and friends, I'd been happier *and* a better rider.

"So, let's get started," Mr. Conner said. "If everyone's warmed up, I want to focus on jumping for this lesson."

Yes! I said to myself.

"During tryouts, I noticed there are a few minor issues with timing," Mr. Conner said. "It's good to be aware of and it's something we can work on—all of us."

Charm and I definitely had issues with that sometimes. During most of our rides, I still had to do a basic move and count strides in my head before we reached a jump. By now, I should have been able to jump without counting strides like a beginner.

"Mike and Doug have assembled a jump course that I want each of you to work over," Mr. Conner said. "You'll each take turns and I want you to do something you learned in beginning riding lessons."

We all looked at each other before turning back to Mr. Conner.

"I want you to count the strides out loud," he said. "I know you're probably thinking that I'm telling you to talk to your horses when riding. But this is an exception."

I liked this idea.

"While you count out loud," Mr. Conner continued. "I'll be taking notes and writing it down if you call out the stride at the wrong time."

Maybe I *didn't* like this idea so much now.

I didn't want anyone to hear me counting out loud and making mistakes. It wasn't as if anyone—like Callie— would say anything out loud about my ride, but I'd be wondering the entire time what she'd be thinking.

"Sasha," Mr. Conner said. "I'd like you and Charm to go first."

I gulped.

"Okay," I said, in that squeaky tone I hated.

"The course is straightforward and, as part of our exercise, I don't want you to walk it first. All of the jumps are

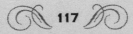

not any higher than anything you've jumped previously. It's more about timing than about difficulty. Don't rush, just take your time and remember that I want to hear your counting."

I nodded and readied myself in the saddle. Mr. Conner's comment about not rushing made me feel as if I could take a second to ready myself. I made sure the stirrups were on the balls of my feet. Then I adjusted the reins in my hands. The extra seconds made me feel more comfortable and ready to tackle the ten jumps.

"I'm ready," I said.

And I meant it. Charm could do this.

Mr. Conner stepped to the side of the arena and the rest of the horses and riders followed him. I blocked out everyone watching me. After enough lessons and shows, I was finally able to forget that people, even Callie, were watching.

I started Charm at a trot, keeping him away from the jumps. I let him into a canter and took him through two circles, making sure he was settled, before allowing him to move toward the first jump. With an even stride, and both ears flicking back at me, Charm glided toward the first red and white striped vertical that wasn't higher than three feet—an easy start to our ride.

In that second, I knew I'd done the right thing with the circles and with settling him before we'd started. We were both less nervous and more comfortable—his body language said it all.

"Start counting," Mr. Conner reminded me.

Oops.

"Seven," I said.

"Louder," Mr. Conner called. "I want to hear you, Sasha. You won't throw off Charm, don't worry. He's used to noise from the crowds at shows."

"Six," I said, raising my voice.

"Good," Mr. Conner said.

"Five, four, three, two," I said. I started to prepare myself for the jump.

"One, *now!*" The last word came out louder than anything I'd said.

At the right moment, Charm gathered himself, rocked back on his haunches and prepared to clear the jump. I lifted slightly out of the saddle and eased my hands a few inches forward along his neck. Charm flew over the vertical, landing with what I was sure were several inches behind us—his back hooves not even coming close to hitting the rail.

Charm hadn't even reacted to my counting. I'd been

sort of worried that my voice would distract him, but he was such a calm horse—he didn't seem to notice anything out of the ordinary.

"Excellent," Mr. Conner called. "Keep it up!"

The next vertical, white with gold stripes that sparkled in the sunlight, was higher than the first by a couple of inches.

"Four, three, two, one, now!" I counted aloud.

Charm pushed off from the ground, recognizing the extra height in this jump. He was the right distance from the rails and, again, we were in no danger of knocking the rail.

We landed safely on the other side and I was in the zone—completely focused and not even aware of anything but Charm and the eight obstacles we had left to go.

I counted strides to the double oxer with faux flower boxes on the sides and the yellow flowers didn't even catch Charm's attention.

We made our way over two more verticals, both a striking cobalt blue, that were spaced close together, and I forgot that I was counting aloud. This exercise was one of my favorites, and probably the most beneficial to me as a rider. I knew I'd be doing it on my own, too.

Charm and I started a sweeping half turn around the arena. His canter was flowing and smooth. I sat easily to

his smooth stride—summers of riding bareback through the pastures had paid off.

We finished the circle and the extra time gave us room for the double oxer we were approaching. By a notch, I let Charm increase his speed to get enough room to make it over the spread. On either side of the oxer, white trellises had fake ivy weaving in and out.

"Five," I said. "Four, three, two, one, now!"

On *now*, Charm moved back on his haunches and he tucked his knees under his body. The extra speed gave him enough of a boost to make it over the spread.

Oxers were one of my fave jumps. There was no other feeling like the suspension in the air. Clichéd or not, it really did feel like flying.

The jump ended so fast—it was too much fun! Charm landed with a soft thud on the other side and I let him keep up his speed as he made his way toward the next vertical. This one had plastic board with orange swirls on the sides. The swirls, meant to throw off the horse, didn't even cause Charm to pause.

We cleared the vertical without a problem, trying not to get too excited, I realized we only had two jumps left—a faux stone wall and a final vertical.

The faux brick stone wall wasn't too high. I counted

the strides and Charm leapt the wall without a problem. *He* didn't know the wall was fake, but he trusted me to get him over the "bricks" safely.

We landed and I cheered in my head. One more left!

"Four, three, two, one, now!" I counted. I knew I'd made a mistake the second I lifted out of the saddle a half second too early.

Charm, always eager to rush the last jump, left the ground on "one" instead of "now" and he wasn't ready. I'd caused him to leave too late.

It was no surprise when I heard the *click* of Charm's hooves against the top railing. He landed and it tumbled behind us, the plastic piping thudding against the ground.

I frowned with disappointment, but patted Charm's neck. He'd done an amazing job—listening to everything I'd told him. The final jump had been my mistake—I knew about his history with rushing final fences and I'd let my enthusiasm about the end of the ride cost us a knocked rail.

I let him canter for a few more strides, then slowed him to a trot before turning him back to Mr. Conner and the rest of the YENT team.

Mr. Conner finished making final notes on his

clipboard, his black Bic pressing into the paper before he looked up at me.

"What did you think about counting aloud?" he asked.

"It was really helpful," I said. "I still do it in my head and to hear myself count out loud was helpful."

"Why was it helpful?" Mr. Conner asked.

I paused, then decided the only way to help myself was to be honest. "Because it made me feel less embarrassed about being on the YENT and still counting strides in my head."

"Sasha," Mr. Conner said. "This," and his gestured around the arena with his hand, "is an embarrassment free-zone. You're all here learning together. And, specifically to the issue of you feeling as though you shouldn't be counting strides, *many* riders at higher levels than you still count in their heads. You're a talented jumper and I want you to feel comfortable using whatever method works for you."

"Thank you," I said. I finally glanced at the other girls. Callie wasn't smirking or looking happy about my mistake. Heather had her ever-present *you'll do better next time or else* look, which was oddly comforting. Brit, smiling, mouthed, *good job*.

Thanks, I mouthed back before looking at Mr. Conner.

Mr. Conner smiled at me. "The counting to yourself has obviously worked. I didn't see any instances of timing problems except for the final jump, which you're aware of. We know Charm has a history of rushing jumps."

"It was my fault," I said. "I got excited that there was only one jump left. My brain knew about Charm's history with final jumps, but I let my own feelings get in the way. He was already primed to go early and I let him."

"That's one issue that you'll both continue to work on," Mr. Conner said. "Charm responds well to you, Sasha, so I don't foresee this becoming a major issue. If, in the future, Charm stops listening and rushes no matter how much we've worked with him, we'll start on a new strategy. Okay?"

"That sounds great," I said. "Thank you."

Mr. Conner glanced over to Callie. "Ready?"

Callie nodded. "Ready."

By the tone of her voice, I knew this was going to be a ride that would captivate everyone's attention. Callie was *on*.

And I was right.

Callie counted out the timing before the ten jumps and didn't miss a stride. She rode as if she were testing for the YENT.

I glanced at Brit and, I swear, ESP passed between us. I wished I'd been able to ride with my BlackBerry

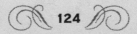

because Brit and I needed a BBM convo right N-O-W.

Mr. Conner discussed Callie's ride, pointing out a mistake I hadn't even seen.

Then Heather rode. She and Aristocrat swept around the course, both horse and rider in unison. I tried to take in every bit of what Heather was doing from the way she timed the jumps to how Aristocrat responded to her cues. If I had to choose among Callie, Brit, or Heather as the best rider—I couldn't.

And, in that moment, reality hit me.

Each rider had been chosen because no one was supposed to be able to distinguish who was better. From my place atop Charm's back, I realized this was the *final* YENT team.

Callie.

Brit.

Heather.

And me.

After Brit had finished her ride, which only solicited a couple of comments from Mr. Conner, he talked to us as a group about how we'd done. Even though I'd rushed the final jump, I was still proud of my ride.

12

THE JACOB EFFECT

"PUT IT IN PERSPECTIVE," BRIT SAID AS WE walked out of the arena together. "You knocked *one* rail after being so nervous. For your first YENT practice with Callie, you did an amazing job."

"Thanks," I said. "That means a lot. Your ride was fantastic, Brit."

Brit smiled, ducking her head a little. "Thanks, Sash. Apollo is a great horse. He makes everything easy."

"He's a fantastic horse," I said. "His—"

I stopped midsentence.

"Sash?"

Brit followed my gaze. Across the lawn, Eric and Jacob stood just feet apart.

Talking.

"Omigodom...

lutely no way this is go...

Hate! What could they poss...

going to end with campus securit...

"It's okay, it's okay," Brit said.

bonded in a class or during a sport or somet...

I rubbed my forehead so hard, I was sure all

makeup had come off. Brit pulled down my hand.

"Maybe they're talking about football?" Brit offered.

"Eric hates football!"

"Um, maybe they're talking about horses?"

"Jacob is terrified of horses!"

"School, then," Brit said. "They've got to have something in common with classes or something."

I saw Jacob shift on his heels and I couldn't take it
anymore.

"I have to go over there," I said.

"Sash—" Brit started to reach for my arm, but there
wasn't any need. I stopped, watching Jacob and Eric fist
bump (*such a dude thing*). Then they walked away from each
other.

That was it for me.

"Meet you in our room?" I asked Brit.

"See you there," she said.

...the courtyard toward Jacob.

"...s everything okay?" I asked. "What's going on? You *never* talk to Eric."

Jacob took my hand. "Everything is totally fine, Sash. I promise. Let's sit for a second."

Still holding Jacob's hand, I followed him over to a wooden bench a few feet off the sidewalk.

My knees bounced when we sat down. I couldn't imagine what he had to talk to Eric about.

"I got Eric's e-mail from the school directory," Jacob said.

"Um, why?"

Jacob put his hand on my knee, calming my bouncing. "I needed to apologize to him. He . . . actually is a decent guy and I was wrong at your party. Eric deserved to hear an explanation from me."

"And he agreed to meet you right away?" I asked.

Jacob nodded. "He e-mailed me back a couple of hours later saying he would meet me."

"Why didn't you tell me?"

"I wanted to make sure he'd show," Jacob said. "I didn't want you to get excited about the possibility of us getting together and then have something go wrong during our talk."

"I would have done the same. What did he say?"

Jacob rubbed my palm. "At first, he just listened. After I talked, he said he appreciated me coming to him and then said if I ever hurt you, there would be a problem."

"And what did you say?" I rubbed my other hand on my breeches.

"That there would never be a problem because I'd never hurt you," Jacob said. I'd never seen such intensity in his eyes.

"You don't have to tell me everything, but I just want to know . . . how did things end?"

Jacob ran his thumb across my cheek. When his hand was back in my lap, it felt as if there was still a warm spot from where he'd touched me.

"You can ask me anything you want, Sasha. We agreed that the past was just that and it was time to move forward. It's a waste of our time and energy to avoid and antagonize each other."

"Really? That's great!" If I tried to stand now, I felt as if I'd collapse into the ground. This was beyond a major relief in my life. Just having Jacob and Eric agree to coexist was a huge deal that I *never* expected.

I scooted closer on the bench, giving Jacob a quick kiss. "Thank you so much, Jacob. You have no idea how much stress this takes off me. I know it couldn't have been easy to talk to him like that. This is one of the nicest things anyone has ever done for me."

And it was. Eric and Jacob had been enemies, with understandable reasons, but the fact that they were able to come to an agreement not to fight meant so much."

"I'd do anything to go back and fix what I did," Jacob said. "And talking to Eric was just the beginning."

I stared at him, tilting my head. "What does that mean?"

"Eric asked me for a favor," Jacob said. "He asked me for help."

"Help? With what?"

"Eric told me he knew that I'm good at math," Jacob said. "He wondered if, as part of our moving forward, if I'd tutor him for a while just to get him on track. He said his grade in the class was so low that he was in danger going on academic probation."

"Oh my God," I said. "That's awful! How did you feel about him asking you?"

"Like it was a good step forward," Jacob said. "Which is why I said yes."

For seconds, I just looked at him, unable to find the words. "That was beyond generous of you, Jacob. It was

more than enough that you apologized to him, but to also tutor him? I can't even find the words to thank you."

And Jacob didn't wait for me to find them. He touched his lips to mine and The Jacob Effect made all of my worries and anxiety about school, riding—everything—go away.

We sat on the bench for a few more minutes before Jacob looked at me. "Want to go to The Sweet Shoppe?" he asked. "I haven't been there in forever. And by forever, I mean for two days."

I giggled. "I'd love to."

"Do you want to invite Brit?" Jacob asked as we stood. "I'd like to get to know your roommate."

"That's a great idea. I'm sure she'll be up for it. Give me an hour to shower, change, and get ready and then we'll meet you there. Okay?"

"Perfect. See you there."

THREE ROOT BEER FLOATS

JACOB HEADED TO BLACKWELL, HIS DORM HALL, and I pulled out my BlackBerry. I couldn't even wait five minutes to talk to Brit.

Sasha Silver:

Be there in 5. You up for The Sweet Shoppe in, like, an hr?"

Brit wrote back right away.

Brit Chan:

Def! But WHAT happened with Jacob? I need details! Dying over here!!

Sasha Silver:

I've got to tell you in person, but srsly, you won't believe it. It was actually something good. Well, better than good.

Brit Chan:

!!! Hurry and get here. We need to talk!!

Sasha Silver:

LOL. I'm at the Orchard stairs. C u in sec.

I stepped around students in the hallway, eager to get to my room. But the Halloween decorations caught my attention. Brit was probably going crazy in our room waiting for me, but I couldn't help it. And she understood. Halloween was both of our favorite holiday.

Even though I saw Orchard a zillion times a week, the decorations that Stephanie, the dorm monitor, and a few of the student council members had put up always made me slow down.

The glass doorway had an intricate spiderweb drawn on it with shimmery white paint. A silver spider sat in the middle of the web. I pulled open the door and all down the hallway, ghosts, bats, and spiders hung on invisible fishing line from the ceiling.

Just before the common room, a giant black cat with an arched tail and fur ruffled up its back was on the wall. Its green eyes were an eerie shade—a mix between green and yellow—and they seemed to follow me down the hallway.

Since Halloween was only days away, almost everyone's door was decorated. Some students had placed plastic pumpkins outside of their door on end tables. Other students had decorated their doors with black

and orange crepe paper. More and more decorations were added every day.

And, just before I reached our room, I looked at the long espresso-colored end table that was always decorated for the appropriate season or holiday. The end table had a beaded pumpkin placemat in the middle and a black bowl with candy off to the side. I always swiped a Kit Kat for me and a pack of SweeTarts for Brit whenever I walked by. I loved the tall candles at the end of each table. The black candles, covered in silver spiderweb paint, were separated by a dozen orange votives in glass holders. I couldn't wait for all of the candles to be lit on Halloween night.

I stopped staring at everything, remembered that Brit was waiting, and slid my key into our door. Just as I started to turn the knob, our whiteboard caught my attention. In bubble letters, Brit had written HAPPY HALLOWEEN! at the top in orange and black dry-erase markers. Under that, over a dozen people had written notes to us.

Boo! Xoxo ~Kristen

Have a "spooktacular" (I know it's cheesy!) Halloween, Sasha and Brit! ~Steph

Trick or Treat! <3, Devon

People had written notes on Paige's and my whiteboard before, but never anything like this. And never so fast!

I read a few more of the comments and looked at some of the holiday-centered doodles before I opened the door. Brit almost knocked me over the second I walked in. She grabbed my hand and pulled me onto the edge of my bed.

"What *happened*?" she asked. "It feels like you took hours to get here! Did they get into a fight? Was everything okay?"

"You won't believe this," I said. "Jacob went to Eric to apologize."

"What?! Seriously?"

"I know! I almost thought I'd heard Jacob wrong when he told me."

"So, Jacob apologized to Eric for kissing you at your birthday party?"

I nodded. "Yep. And they decided the past wasn't worth fighting about anymore."

"No. Way." Brit leaned back on her elbows. "Wow. That's huge, Sash. Guys *never* do that."

"I know. I kept waiting for Jacob to say that something had gone wrong with their conversation, but he didn't. And guess what?"

"There *can't* be more." Brit said up straight, her long hair flipping over her shoulders.

"Oh, but there is. And it's big. Eric told Jacob he was having problems with math this semester. He said he'd

heard Jacob was good in math and wondered if he'd tutor him for a little while. Otherwise, if Eric's grade dropped any lower, he'd be on academic probation."

"Did Jacob say yes?"

"He did. He thought it was a good way to show that they could put old feelings behind them instead of just talk about it."

Brit clasped her hands together. "That's *so* great! You must be ridiculously excited to have them not fighting anymore."

I flopped back against my bed. "You have no idea. It would have been more than enough if Jacob had apologized to Eric, but tutoring him is just amazing. He really is showing me that he meant what he said about making things work out between them."

"I'm really, really happy for you," Brit said. "We should get ice cream or something."

I laughed. "It's funny you said that. Jacob invited both of us to The Sweet Shoppe in about an hour, if you're up for it. He wants to meet you and get to know my roomie."

Brit smiled. "I'd love to! That sounds like so much fun."

We kept chatting, there never being a moment of silence between us, while we took our showers, did makeup, and got dressed superfast.

I'd chosen black skinny jeans, a supersoft pink shirt with a charcoal hoodie, and a pair of silver ballet flats.

Brit, always chic, had paired flared jeans with tall boots and a white cable-knit sweater.

"Accessories and then we're out of here," I said.

Brit held up the light pink Caboodles box that we used to store our jewelry.

I grabbed a pair of skinny black hoops and Brit chose a pair of faux diamond hearts. We finished and left Orchard, heading for The Sweet Shoppe.

When we got there, Jacob was already waiting with a table for three. He stood, smiling at us. I waved at him, smiling.

"Hey, guys," Jacob said.

I looked at Brit. "Brit, this is Jacob Schwartz. I'm so glad you guys can finally meet."

"It's nice to meet you," Jacob said to Brit, smiling at her.

"You too," Brit said. "Thanks for inviting me."

We all sat down and the waitress came over to see what we wanted to drink.

"Go ahead," Jacob said.

"I'd like a root beer float, please," I said.

"That sounds so good. I'll have one, too," Brit said.

"Make that three," Jacob said.

The waitress nodded at us and left our table.

"Sasha told me you're on the YENT," Jacob said. "It's cool that you're roommates and you ride together. Do you like Canterwood so far?"

I loved that Jacob was asking Brit about riding. He didn't know anything about it except for what I'd told him about Charm and riding when we'd first met. Jacob had spent a few hours in the stable when we'd filmed a documentary for Mr. Ramirez's film class last year.

There was an immediate smile on Brit's face. "I love it! I almost passed out when I got accepted. I ran from the mailbox to my kitchen and screamed to my parents that I'd made it."

Jacob laughed, but not in a mean way. "I almost did the same thing. Well, I probably *would* have if my parents hadn't been at the neighbor's barbeque."

We all laughed.

The waitress came with our root beer floats and set them on the pale blue table. "I'll be back in a while to see if you want anything else," she said.

We thanked her and dug long spoons into the tasty vanilla ice cream.

"What're you interested in?" Brit asked Jacob. "Sasha told me that you play football and like video games."

Jacob reached under the table and squeezed my hand as if surprised that I'd talked to my roommate about him.

"Football's fun," Jacob said. "I'm not great at it, but I like working out. I'm at the media center, though, every second I get a chance. I love playing games—Nintendo's my favorite."

I took a sip of root beer and glanced over, seeing four seventh graders sitting two tables in front of us. One blond girl facing me was wearing something that looked so familiar . . . it was Brit's tan jacket with beautiful clear buttons.

I shook my head, annoyed at myself for thinking the girl was trying to emulate Brit. That was just coincidence.

But then . . . I saw two girls get up and walk to the counter. They had the boots I'd bought in Manhattan when I'd stayed with Heather during fall break. Were they . . . copying me? Copying us?

Oh my God, I said to myself. *You're ridiculous. Maybe someone would copy Brit, but definitely not you.* I went back to joining in the conversation between Brit and Jacob.

And easy chatter among us didn't cease through root beer floats or fudge brownies. Brit had this ability to make everyone like her and I couldn't have been happier that my new friend and my boyfriend liked each other.

14

HALLOWEEN IS THE PERFECT TIME FOR A GHOST INVITATION

"HE'S SOOO GREAT, SASH!" BRIT SAID, squeezing my arm. We'd just split up from Jacob and were walking back to our room.

"I'm glad you like him," I said. "Jacob's just . . ." I paused. "He's just Jacob. We had things, people—both of us included—mess up the start of what could have been something amazing. But *now* we have a real chance at trying."

Brit ran her hand through her long hair, flicking it over her shoulder. "Just take this for what it is—a fresh start."

I breathed in the crisp air, taking in all of my favorite scents of fall. Apples. Burning wood. Cider. It *was* a new start with Jacob and things were on the right track so far, especially after our first date.

For the rest of the walk Brit and I talked about boys.

"I haven't been here long enough to really do anything but look at boys," Brit said. "But, trust me, I've been looking."

We giggled.

"There's nothing wrong with looking. There are tons of cute guys here. It *definitely* doesn't hurt to check out your future options."

I almost skipped beside Brit as I pulled opened the door to Orchard. We stepped inside, both pretend-shrieking as the fake bloody hand in the giant green bowl of candy inside the doorway reached up, sensing our motion.

Our laughter stopped the second we saw Callie.

"Sasha," Callie said.

Her dark brown eyes locked on mine and I couldn't imagine what she was about to say.

"I want to talk," she continued.

I wondered if I'd heard her right or if my brain, in Halloween mode, was playing tricks on me and making me see a ghost Callie.

I blinked and she was still there.

"Um, sure," I said, my voice quiet. "What's going on?"

"I want to talk—*alone.*"

Brit shifted beside me and smiled at Callie and me.

"I'm going to get started on homework or I'll never fin-ish," Brit said. "Sasha, see you back in our room."

I nodded, wanting her to stay but knowing I had to take this chance to talk to Callie.

Brit walked away from us and I heard our door shut down the hallway. I hadn't been alone with Callie in *forever.*

"I'm don't want to drag this out," Callie said, folding her arms. "So I'm just going to say it."

I looked behind Callie at the pumpkin stickers that Stephanie had put on the WELCOME TO ORCHARD message board. I needed something, anything, to keep me from fainting.

"Go ahead," I said.

"You, Paige, and I need to talk," Callie said.

"About what?"

Callie shook her head. "Please, Sasha. You already know."

I didn't want to stand here anymore and play this game. Sure, I knew she wanted to talk about the Jacob situation, but I didn't know how specific. But if we all sat down, maybe I had a shot at ending our weird relationship.

"Fine. When and where?"

Callie seemed a surprised, and maybe a little unpre-pared, that I'd agreed so easily.

"Let me talk to Paige and find a time and day when she's free," Callie said. "I'll text you."

And, just like the ghost I'd first thought she might have been, Callie slipped out of the doors, leaving me alone in the hallway.

15

A SPOOKY
ANNOUNCEMENT

AFTER CLASS AND MY RIDING LESSON ON
Friday, the only thing I wanted to do was spend time
with Charm. I especially loved being in the stable now,
since it was only a week before Halloween. Mike, Doug,
and Mr. Conner had decorated the stable—keeping
hairy plastic spiders and giant rats far out of the horses'
reach.

But before I could spend time with Charm, there was
a stablewide meeting in the indoor arena. I imagined that
Mr. Conner wanted to talk to us about the upcoming fall
schedule, but I wasn't sure.

In the already half-full arena, I stood near the back of
the crowd.

"Boo!"

I jumped, whirling around. Troy, Ben, and Andy laughed, their faces red as they stood behind me.

I crossed my arms over my chest, pretending to be mad. "Seriously, guys? Was that the best you could do?"

Dropping the act, I smiled at them at them, plotting in my head a way to scare them later. I saw Eric enter the arena with Rachel and her friends. Julia and Alison were near the center of the arena. I looked for Heather's blond head, but didn't see her standing with them. She must have been late. The Trio was, well, the Trio. They were always together.

"Sasha, hey."

I looked over at Brit as she stepped beside me.

"Any idea what this is about?" I asked her.

"Not a clue. You?"

"None."

Brit craned her neck, staring across the campus. "What's Heather doing over there?" she asked.

"Heather? Where?" I looked back toward the Trio, thinking I'd somehow missed Heather joining them. But Brit pointed toward the back of the room where Heather was standing.

With Troy.

The two had separated from the rest of the guys and were standing close.

The clique leader wasn't with her girls. This was so weird.

"You know she's with Troy," I said. "I'm sure she offered to hang with Julia and Alison, but they told her to go with Troy."

But I wasn't so sure if that was really true or not. All three members of the infamous Trio hadn't been together much, recently.

I'd seen Julia at the movies with Ben.

Alison had been working with Sunstruck.

Heather had been with Troy or riding Aristocrat on her own.

But the Trio would never break up. They were *the* force on campus. Just because they were spending some time with other people instead of being linked at the arms didn't mean anything.

The chatter in the arena silenced when Mr. Conner entered. He stood in the front of the arena and looked around at us. We stared back and the room seemed filled with uneasiness.

"Everyone can relax," Mr. Conner said. "This isn't an announcement about changes to stable policies or anything that you need to be nervous about."

Whew.

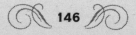

"But," Mr. Conner said with a smile. "Some of you might get a little spooked after you leave. As you all know, next Sunday is Halloween. The stable will contribute an open, campus-wide activity for all, and, as a treat for you, I've planned something special."

Brit and I looked at each other. This type of announcement was definitely a kind Mr. Conner needed to make more often.

"As our part in the day of Halloween festivities," Mr. Conner said, "we'll be providing fun snacks and drinks in the gazebo, which will be decorated to fit the occasion."

That sounded like so much fun! In my head, I was already running through Halloween-themed snacks and beverages like orange soda and chocolate cupcakes.

"You will get *your* reward at nightfall," Mr. Conner said.

Everyone started to murmur, trying to figure out what it could be.

"When the sun sets, come to the stable and tack up your horses. Mike, Doug, and I will be leading a haunted trail ride."

"Omigod!" Brit and I whispered at the same time.

"No way!" someone in the arena said.

"Sooo cool," said a girl.

"None of you will be allowed on the trails starting

tomorrow. I will be determining a safe path and installing lighting and a few surprises along the way. Everyone needs to stay out of the woods; otherwise it won't be a surprise. Deal?"

"Deal!" we all said in unison.

"Good." Mr. Conner laughed at our reaction. "Have a good weekend and I'll see many of you for lessons on Monday."

What had been a low murmur when Mr. Conner entered the arena ratcheted up to full out excitement as students streamed out the openings.

"The trail ride is going to be sooo cool!" I said.

"I thought the gazebo party was enough," Brit said. "And then he surprised us with that. It's going to be the best Halloween ever."

"I'm excited to spend it with Charm," I said. "He's going to have just as much fun."

"You're going to hang out with him for a little while, right?" Brit asked.

"Yeah," I said. "This week has been so crazy. I've either been hanging out with Jacob, doing homework, or a zillion other things. I think he misses me."

Brit smiled. "I'm sure he misses you. Go hang with your boy. See you later in our room."

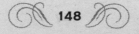

I walked back down the aisle toward Charm's stall. He'd been perfect during our lesson earlier and he deserved some one-on-one time. In cross-ties just before Charm's stall, Aristocrat was standing still as Heather groomed him.

"Did you forget that we just finished our lesson a couple of hours ago?" I teased.

Heather rolled her eyes. "Please. We've got major shows coming up. I need to practice."

I walked up to Aristocrat and rubbed his neck. "Are you going to let showing take over your life again?"

I wanted to take back the question the second it came out of my mouth, afraid Heather would snap at me, but it was too late.

"No," she said. There wasn't any anger in her voice. She lifted Aristocrat's saddle onto his back and reached under his stomach for the girth. Straightening, she looked at me. "I'm not doing that again."

Unclipping Aristocrat's cross-ties, I slid his reins over his head, starting to bridle him. Heather didn't object to my help.

"I have this new thing with Troy," Heather said. "And I'm trying to figure it out. Plus, with school and everything else, there's not enough time for me to be here twenty-four seven anymore even if I wanted to."

"So you're riding when you can," I said. "I get that—totally. I really do think that when you only have a limited amount of time to be at the stable, you work that much harder to get done what you need in a shorter amount of time than it used to take."

"Maybe, Silver. But don't think for a second that it doesn't mean we're not all going to be ready for the first big show of the season. We're going to win—easily."

I grinned. *That* was Heather Fox.

"No doubt," I said.

I finished bridling Aristocrat, then waved good-bye to Heather. I walked a few steps before I turned back to her.

"Can I practice with you?"

"As long as you don't get in my way," Heather said, smiling sweetly.

"I'll be there in a few minutes."

I walked down the aisle to Charm's stall, smiling at the ghost decal Mr. Conner had let me put up on his door.

"Hi, boy," I said.

I let myself into the stall and he walked right into my arms. I hugged him tight—loving the scent of hay and sweet grain that clung to his body.

"I came for some Sasha-Charm time," I said. "But Heather's willing to practice with us. It okay with you

if we hang out together after a little more riding?"

Charm seemed to understand my question. He bobbed his head. That was my boy—game for anything.

"Be right back," I said. I grabbed his tack and it only took us minutes to get ready. His coat was already clean from the last lesson and, within fifteen minutes, we were walking down the aisle to practice with Heather.

The big door to the exit was still open and dusk was settling over campus. I jumped sideways a little when one of the plastic skeletons hanging from the ceiling moved when a breeze blew through the stable. Laughing to myself, I put on my helmet and walked into the arena. I had something *much* bigger to be worried about.

Heather.

16

JUST GOSSIP

CHARM AND I WEREN'T EVEN FIVE MINUTES into our practice session with Heather when I realized the goriest, scariest haunted house would be less scary than this.

"Silver, your hands are ridiculous," Heather said. "I know you're, like, afraid of me but stop shaking."

"Ha, ha," I said. "My hands *aren't* shaking." And they weren't—but they were bouncing around Charm's neck.

Heather and I had put the horses through a light warm-up before starting our private practice session. Instead of focusing on dressage or jumping, we'd decided flatwork was a basic place to start and a good way to end the week.

"Take Charm though another spiral," Instructor Heather called. She'd halted Aristocrat in the center of the arena and, with the reins resting on his neck, was gesturing at me.

I couldn't *wait* to coach her next.

Charm and I started the pattern—the circle getting smaller with each rotation. I kept him at a posting trot and focused on keeping each rotation even.

When Charm's body felt as if it started to strain, I stopped, turning him in the opposite direction and made another spiral.

"Nice," Heather said.

I looked up, hopeful she'd say that she was ready for me to coach her now. I patted Charm's neck.

"Ready to swap places?" I asked.

Heather laughed. She moved Aristocrat forward so that she looked that much more menacing from the top of his back.

"You're not getting off *that* easy, Silver," Heather said. "Who do you think you're talking to?"

"What do you want me to do?" I asked. I wanted to get through this as painless as possible so I could start my weekend.

"Two more spirals," Heather said.

I started to move Charm forward, but Heather raised her hand.

"No stirrups."

Apparently, "painless" wasn't going to be part of my vocabulary during this session.

An hour later, Heather and I had dismounted and were cooling the horses.

Every muscle in my body ached and I couldn't wait to jump in the shower and wash off the day. We groomed the horses together, then started across the now moonlit campus to Orchard.

"What're you doing tonight?" Heather asked.

"I don't know yet," I said. "Brit and I will probably watch a movie or something. You?"

"Troy and I are meeting up later," Heather said, she shook her blond hair out of its ponytail. "We haven't decided what we're doing yet."

"Cool. I'm sure whatever you do, you'll have fun."

And that reminded me to turn on my phone. I'd had it off while I'd been in the stable. As the phone lit up, almost like a flashlight as we walked across campus, it immediately started chiming.

One.

Two.

Three.

Four.

Five times.

All BBMs.

I opened the messenger and saw one was from Jacob and the rest were from Brit.

"*Someone's* popular all of the sudden," Heather said.

But I barely heard her. I'd opened Brit's name first and was scanning her messages over and over.

Brit Chan:

Sash—I know you're w/Charm but you've got 2 BBM me.

Brit Chan:

Srsly. (But don't freak when you read this—it's not an emergency.)

Brit Chan:

Okay. Your phone's def off.

Brit Chan:

If ur not back in half an hr, I'm coming 2 stable.

That last message was fifteen minutes ago.

I opened Jacob's message.

Jacob Schwartz:

Hey, S. U and Brit want 2 grab food @ The Slice 2nite?

I exited out of messenger, not able to type a message to him. Not until I knew what was going on with Brit.

"Something's up," I said to Heather. "Brit BBMed me a bunch of times. I think something big happened when we were riding."

She turned to me. "What're you talking about?"

And then her phone lit up.

She looked at the screen, shaking her head.

"I think I know what Brit messaged you about," Heather said.

We were just yards from Orchard now, walking faster.

"What? How?"

Heather looked at me, chewing on the inside of her lip. "Julia just messaged me."

"So? What did she say?"

I was getting more and more nervous by the second.

"She's with Brit and Alison in our suite," Heather said. She hesitated.

"Heather! Just tell me! You're freaking me out."

Heather sighed. "The gossip blogger struck again."

I almost laughed. "That's it? The *gossip blogger*? Seriously, I thought something awful had happened."

Heather pulled open the door to Orchard, her expression not even close to laughing.

"It did, Sash. To Paige."

"What?"

Dashing forward, I almost left Heather in the hallway as I hurried to the Trio's suite. But she caught up with me and, together, we walked inside where Alison, Julia, and Brit were clustered around Alison's laptop on the coffee table. *It's just gossip, it's just gossip,* I repeated to myself. But that didn't make me any calmer.

I knelt in front of the Mac, my heartbeat out of control as I stared at the page, reading to myself.

It looks as though Manhattan's once-perfect princess Paige Parker has taken a fall from her throne. The poor girl had just gotten every-thing—including her first clichéd knight in shining armor—Ryan Shore.

But this afternoon, the Prince and Princess were caught having a not-so-refined shouting match behind the science building. The verdict? A split among the couple.

I guess not all endings are happily ever after.

</3

The broken heart symbol made me want to cry.

"This—this isn't true," I said. "There's no way."

Julia shrugged from her position on the couch. "It sounds pretty accurate to me. Why else would someone target Paige by name? No one has any motive to go after her."

I sat down on the floor as if I'd been pushed. Brit reached over and put a hand on my shoulder.

"Sash, it really could just be gossip. Someone trying to mess with people."

"It has to be," I said to Brit. "There's no way Paige and Ryan broke up."

Paige and I really weren't speaking, but I didn't care. I had to make sure this wasn't true. And . . . if it was, I'd be on my way to Winchester, if Paige wanted to see me, to support her.

I grabbed my phone, which I'd tossed on the Trio's recliner, and typed a message to Paige.

Sasha Silver:

P? I know things are weird w/us right now, but I don't care. R u ok?

Everyone watched my phone, waiting for Paige to BBM me back.

Almost immediately, a typing signal appeared beside her name. I braced myself.

Paige Parker:

Angry, but totally fine. Ryan and I did NOT break up.

"Omigod, I knew it!" I said, leaning back against the couch.

"Stupid blogger," Alison said. She was curled up under an afghan at the end of the couch. "I don't know why anyone would do something so mean. It's beyond gross."

While everyone started talking, I typed another message to Paige.

Sasha Silver:

I *knew* it. I'm really glad u guys r ok.

Paige Parker:

Thanks, Sasha. I've been getting a million msgs all day. Everyone believed the post!

Sasha Silver:

It sounded so real and, for a sec, I was freaking out 4 u. But I'm so glad ur w/Ryan and everything's ok.

This time, it took Paige a few seconds longer to start another message.

Paige Parker:

Thanks, S. I hope ur doing ok and I'm sure I'll run into you soon.

Sasha Silver:

Def. Bye.

I closed out BBM, feeling a little sad that my conversation with Paige was over.

"I'm happy for her," Heather said, looking at me. "Ryan's a good guy."

"He's perfect for her," I said. "I just wish the gossip blogger would stop. Or that people would stop reading it."

"Good luck with that," Julia said. "Everyone *loves* gossip."

And, unfortunately, I knew she was right.

17
AND THE WEEKEND BEGINS

A FEW MINUTES LATER, BRIT AND I WENT back to our room, both relieved that there was no breakup crisis.

"I was so caught up in the Paige scandal," I said. "That I didn't even BBM Jacob back yet. He messaged me while I was at the stable."

"How was Charm time, anyway?" Brit asked.

I put my riding boots on our mat and started grabbing fresh clothes.

"Heather was at the stable and we decided to coach each other for a little while," I said. "She can make me *crazy*, but you know what a great rider she is. I couldn't pass it up."

"I'm glad you stayed," Brit said. "Nothing exciting

was going on here. I got some homework done—lame for a Friday I know—and then the gossip blog mess went viral. What was Jacob up to? Did he message you about Paige too?"

"Actually, he wanted to know if you and I wanted to grab pizza at The Slice tonight," I said. "Interested?"

"Most definitely," Brit said. "I showered when I got back, so whenever you guys want to meet up works for me."

"Awesome. I'll tell him we're coming."

Sasha Silver:

Hey! Srry I didn't respond right away. Fake crisis—will explain ltr. Brit and I def want 2 do pizza. What time r u free?

I'd just picked out my clothes when my BBM went off.

Jacob Schwartz:

Want to meet in an hr—hr and a half?

Sasha Silver:

Perf! ☺ C u there.

Pizza at The Slice with Jacob and Brit sounded like the best way to start the weekend.

18

AT LEAST YOU'RE NOT A TOTAL LIAR

LATE SATURDAY MORNING, I WAS BACK IN the stable prepping Charm for a practice session with Brit and Heather.

On Charm's tack trunk, my phone buzzed.

It was a text from Callie.

Paige and I can meet u 2nite at 6 at The Sweet Shoppe. U free?

Before I could change my mind, I typed a message back.

6 is perfect. C u there.

Brit, leading a tacked-up Apollo, walked over. "You okay?" she asked.

"Callie wants to talk *tonight* at six," I said. "I'll probably have a panic attack before then."

"No you won't," Brit said. "You're going to be fine. I promise. C'mon." She gestured toward the arena. "Let's keep you busy and start with a riding session."

"Okay." I practically exhaled the word.

I followed Brit down the aisle, feeling sweat already starting to prickle under my shirt.

There was a *looong* way to go till six.

Like a true friend, Brit kept her promise and made sure I was busy all day. We rode, groomed the horses for hours, then watched a couple of movies. By the time the credits rolled on the final film we'd selected, it was five-fifty.

"I better go," I said. "I don't want them to be mad if I'm late."

Brit looked up from her chair where she'd been painting her nails a metallic blue. "You're going to be fine, Sasha. It's doesn't feel like it now, but it's going to be easier in the future if you can all come to some sort of agreement to get along."

"I know you're right," I said. "I'm just going to go and not drag it out."

"BBM or call if you need anything," Brit said.

I slid my purse onto my shoulder. "I will. Thanks."

The walk to The Sweet Shoppe seemed to be the quickest in history. I forced myself to step inside and look around

for Callie and Paige. Both girls were seated at the back in a corner table—the most private spot there.

I slid into a chair across from both of them.

"We ordered three Diet Cokes," Paige said. "I hope that was okay."

"That's great, thank you," I said.

I stared at them for a moment, just waiting.

"Sasha," Callie said. "I want to hear the truth about Jacob and your birthday party from you."

I swallowed, wishing my Coke was here already. "You deserve to hear it from me. Callie, that night, I went into the hallway with Eric so he could give me my present in private. We kissed and Jacob saw us. Eric went back inside and Jacob saw what Eric had given me—a heart charm for my bracelet. He asked me if I really wanted it and I didn't answer him. He was upset and went back inside before I could think of what to say."

I took a breath as our sodas arrived. No one touched theirs—Callie and Paige kept looking at me.

"I knew that Jacob liked me," I continued. "But it made me sick that he was your first boyfriend and you were crazy about him. He . . ." and I *hated* saying this because I knew how much it would hurt. " . . . told me he liked you so, so much, Callie, but that he regretted that he never got a chance with me."

Callie's face didn't move. She didn't look hurt or surprised—just like she wanted to know everything.

"When I blew out my birthday candles, I wished I could fix everything and take back all of the lies I'd told— ones I thought would keep you and Jacob together."

I sipped my Diet Coke. Neither girl said a word. They were really putting me through it, but I deserved it.

"I told Paige I was going to the bathroom, but I really went to my room. I felt like a total fraud. I hated that everyone was celebrating me when I'd been doing such horrible things. I was in my room and Jacob came in. He told me, again, that he knew I was with someone and he was trying to be respectful of that, but that he couldn't stay away."

I shifted in my seat that was started to feel super uncomfortable. "Jacob begged me to admit that I liked him," I said. "I told him no and before I could do anything, he . . . kissed me. I pushed him away and saw Eric standing in the doorway."

I rubbed my forehead, feeling my temple throb. "That's exactly how it happened, Callie. I'm so sorry."

A strange mix of relief and anxiety came over me. Now, Callie knew the truth from me, which she'd deserved since my party. But I had no idea how she'd take it.

Callie took a long sip of Diet Coke, then looked at me. "Well, at least you're still not a total liar since your story matches what I heard in the bathroom during the Homecoming Dance. And what Paige told me."

I almost choked on my soda. It took me at least half a minute before I could say anything. I was surprised not to feel too emotional about Callie. What bothered me the most was Paige.

"You—you overheard Paige and me talking about my party?" I asked.

Callie nodded, taking a casual sip of soda. "Yep. I was in one of the back stalls. A couple of days later, I went to Paige with what I'd heard and asked her to tell me the truth. As my friend, she did."

"I can't believe this," I said. "This whole time, you acted as if I was guilty—like I'd been the one who'd gone after Jacob."

I turned to Paige. "I know I messed up. But you could have told me that Callie already knew. You knew how much I'd *agonized* over that."

Paige blinked rapidly, trying to stop her tears. But she didn't say anything.

I pushed down my emotions about Paige, knowing this wasn't the place to deal with them. I was also determined

not to turn this into yet another drama at The Sweet Shoppe revolving around me.

"Thank you for listening to me," I said. "I'm really, really sorry about how all of this happened. No matter what happens with any of us, I'm just glad that everything is out there now. At least we're all being honest."

And, with that, I got up and left the table.

When I got back to my room, I was exhausted. I gave Brit a brief rundown of what had happened, promising to tell her more later, and fell asleep on top of my comforter before even changing into pajamas.

19

GIMME A "T"! GIMME AN "R"! GIMME AN "O"! "GIMME A "Y"!

LATE SATURDAY AFTERNOON, MY BBM CHIMED.
Heather was on her way back from the gym and I was lying
in bed reading Teen Style.

Heather Fox:

Got a sec 2 chat?

Sasha Silver:

Sure. What's up?

Heather Fox:

1ˢᵗ date w/Troy tonight.

Sasha Silver:

Yaay! ☺ ☺

Heather Fox:

You should try out for cheerleading.

Sasha Silver:

Never mind—maybe u don't want my help . . .

Heather Fox:

U tire me. I'm srs. I'm . . . nervous abt this.

Sasha Silver:

You'll be fine—I promise. Troy really, really likes, you, H. I can tell.

Heather Fox:

Thanks, S. Alison's helping me pick out clothes, so it's distracting.

Sasha Silver:

Fun! I'm sure Julia will help too.

Heather Fox:

Doubt it. She locked herself in her room to do hmwk.

Sasha Silver:

Well, let me know what happens.

I put my phone away, glad to see a hint of the Heather I'd seen and liked during fall break.

20

GOOD NEWS AND BAD

LATER THAT NIGHT, BRIT AND I WERE watching a comedy on TV when her phone beeped. She picked it up, looked at it with one eye on the TV screen and then turned her full attention to the phone.

"Gossip blogger," Brit said. "Grab your computer."

"Not again," I groaned. I opened my laptop and there it was.

So, it seems like the new girl on campus thinks she's the most amazing student to ever to grace Canterwood.

So.

Not.

True!

This small-town girl acts like she's from NYC or LA and has managed to charm everyone with her wide, dark eyes.

But she doesn't have a chance at overtaking the cliques already running this school. New Girl, give up and crawl back home.

"*Who* is doing this?" I asked. "It's awful!"

When I looked over at Brit, her eyes were teary.

"What's wrong?" I asked. "Brit?"

Brit's finger hovered over one sentence. *This small-town girl . . .*

"The blogger is talking about me," Brit said.

"No," I said. "No. They can't be."

But when I read the message again—"small-town" and "wide dark eyes," I knew Brit was right.

And things had finally gone too far.

I calmed Brit and we sent an e-mail to Headmistress Drake with the blog post.

"There," I said, when we pressed send. "That's got to make you feel a little better."

"It does," Brit said, finally smiling again. "Let's watch another movie."

"Done. We'll find the funniest comedy ever made and forget about . . . huh, I already forgot."

That made Brit grin. "I'll start looking for a movie," she said.

I started to follow her, then my phone buzzed and I picked it up. All that was there was a thumbs up symbol from Heather.

I smiled to myself. Sounds like her date had gone better than she'd expected.

21

WORRIED?

WHEN I GOT TO THE STABLE FOR MY AFTER-
noon lesson, everyone was talking. Some students were
whispering, others were yelling down the aisle.

"Everyone!" Mr. Conner's voice boomed down the
aisle. "Indoor arena, now."

I spotted Julia and ran over to her.

"What's going on?" I asked.

"Gossip blogger," she said. "He or she targeted the
Haunted Trail Ride this time."

"No way!"

This was getting to an insane, borderline scary level.
Headmistress Drake had sent out an e-mail to the entire student body warning them that whomever was in charge of the
blog would be suspended and possibly expelled if caught.

I pulled out my phone to look up the blog post.

Do you dare?

Whispers of a haunted trail ride are all over campus. Trails are being marked, decorations are being placed, and lighting is being strung.

But could what's supposed to be a night of harmless fun turn into a nightmare?

Now I understood why Mr. Conner had called this meeting. He strode into the arena, a paper in hand and, scowling, turned to us.

"Whomever is writing these posts should know that they are having no affect on our plans. The Haunted Trail ride will continue as scheduled and it *will* be safe, I assure you."

I'd been worried that he'd cancel the ride.

"Extra security measures for both horse and rider will be put into place. None of you are in any danger and the night will be just as fun as we intended. Now, for those of you who have lessons, please go get your horses ready. We're not giving this blogger any more attention."

As we walked out of the arena, I noticed Julia had already disappeared, leaving Heather and Alison behind.

"You worried?" I asked Heather.

She shook her head. "Nope. Not when Mr. Conner's involved."

22

NOW, THIS IS HALLOWEEN!

"HAPPY HALLOWEEN!" THE SENTIMENTS had been called across campus all day. Since the holiday had fallen on a Sunday this year, the school had made the *entire* day Halloween themed.

We'd started the morning with a "Spook-Tacular" breakfast. The menu choices were insane. Pumpkin muffins with faces on them, peeled grapes, and pancakes with chocolate chips stuck in them to look like eyes, mouth, and teeth.

I spent breakfast with Jacob, did a little homework and talked to my parents, then met Brit for a "gory" lunch. Brit chose tomato soup and I picked spaghetti with sauce.

But all day, I was counting down the hours to the gazebo party and the Haunted Trail ride. The school had filled the day with optional Halloween activities from horror movie screenings to storytelling around the campfire. Brit and I watched *Scream* together at the media center then spent the rest of the afternoon watching scary-but-funny movies like *Hocus Pocus* and *It's the Great Pumpkin, Charlie Brown.* It was my favorite Hallowwen movie that I watched every year. I owned it on DVD, but still watched it every time a station aired it during October.

Finally it was time to get ready. Brit and I dressed for the occasion. I pulled on an orange hoodie and black breeches. Brit chose blood red breeches and a black sweater. Almost too excited to talk, we walked down to the lake and saw orange and purple twinkly lights decorating the gazebo.

"I can't wait to get there!" I said.

Brit nodded. "Me too. It looks sooo amazing!"

We reached the giant wooden gazebo and it was overflowing with riders and students who weren't from the stable.

Mr. Conner, Mike, and Doug had outdone themselves with decorations. If they'd done this much with the gazebo, I couldn't imagine how the trail ride was going to look. I'd BBMed Jacob to meet me there and he said he couldn't wait.

Brit and I walked up the stairs, tilting our heads back

to look at the ceiling that had a cluster of orange and black lights that came down in strands and were tied to the railing. Eerie music with howling wolves, cackling witches, and flapping bat wings played softly in the background.

A circular table in the middle held chips, dip, soda (lots of orange), cookies made from every cookie cutter possible, and cupcakes with Halloween themed toppers and sprinkles. Immediately, I reached for an orange plate and picked up a chocolate cupcake with a ghost on it.

"Starting without me, huh?"

I turned to see Jacob.

"Hi!" I threw my arms around him. It felt so good to share my favorite holiday with him.

"Let's party!" Jacob said.

And we did. We stuffed our faces with at least one of everything and downed cups of orange soda.

I went back for another mini-cupcake, hoping I could find room, and spotted Julia and Alison talking to Ben. Even though she was with her boyfriend, Julia had a scowl on her face. I wondered if they were having a problem. But where was . . . there. Heather and Troy had found a private spot in the gazebo and were standing close, whispering in each other's ears. I loved seeing them together. Heather deserved to have a guy in her life and Troy was a good one.

Mr. Conner stepped into the gazebo all dressed in black. "The Haunted Trail ride begins in twenty minutes for anyone who would like to participate."

Jacob pulled me into a hug, putting his lips close to my ear. "I wish we could have spent more of the night together."

"Me too. I had an amazing time with you."

And, under the twinkle of the lights, Jacob gave me my first Halloween kiss.

LIKE A LOSER

BACK AT THE STABLE, THE HORSES WERE already tacked up. I mounted Charm and led him out of the stable.

"Happy Halloween, boy," I said. "We're going on a special trail ride. Are you excited?"

Charm nodded.

Laughing, I patted his neck and mounted.

We waited for all of the riders to gather in front of the stable. The Trio and Brit rode up beside Charm and me. Mike, Doug, and Mr. Conner joined us.

"If you're all ready, let's go," Mr. Conner said. "Stick to the lighted path *only* and if you feel your horse or yourself getting nervous about any of the surroundings, please speak up and Mike or Doug will escort you back to the stable."

"Like a loser," Heather whispered.

We got into line and followed Mr. Conner. I was behind Brit with Heather, Julia, and Alison following me.

Immediately, I noticed the black lanterns with candles inside that looked like real flames.

"Wow," I whispered to myself.

The entire path was lined on either side with orange twinkly lights. Skeletons, ghosts, and witches hung from various tree branches. Mr. Conner had made sure everything was at the right level so it wouldn't spook any of the horses.

A zombie walked in front of us, weaving around the horses, and everyone laughed. This was scary-silly and I loved it.

"Hey," said a familiar voice. Eric rode by, waving back at me as he passed us on Luna to catch up to his friend. "Happy Halloween."

"You too," I called.

The trail widened and I turned to Brit to say how much fun this was. But Brit wasn't beside me.

A rider, all dressed in black, with a crimson colored mask over his face, rode toward me.

Omigod, omigod! The gossip blogger was actually right!

I started to scream, but I froze.

"Don't be scared," said a voice I knew. "I just wanted to say Happy Halloween again."

The rider pulled off his mask.

"Jacob?"

He grinned back at me, the moon and the lighting casting shadows on his face.

"How did you—what are you doing out here? And you're riding!"

I couldn't believe what I was seeing.

"Well, Eric and I *might* have told you a little white lie," Jacob said. "Remember how we were tutoring?"

I nodded, still confused.

"Well, it had nothing to do with math. Eric was tutoring, well, I guess *teaching* me about riding. He taught me enough so that I'd be able to go on this trail ride with you."

"I can't believe you did this! You're *terrified* of horses and you're out here at night."

"I did it for you, Sash. I wanted this to be an amazing Halloween."

I leaned toward him, so our faces were close. "This is the *perfect* Halloween."

And for the second time on Halloween, we kissed.

ABOUT THE AUTHOR

Twenty-three-year-old Jessica Burkhart is a writer from New York City. Like Sasha, she's crazy about horses, lip gloss, and all things pink and sparkly. Jess was an equestrian and had a horse like Charm before she started writing. To watch Jess's vlogs and read her blog, visit www.jessicaburkhart.com.

Jammed full of surprises!

LiP SMACKER.
LOUNGE

FIVE GIRLS. ONE ACADEMY. AND SOME SERIOUS ATTITUDE.

CANTERWOOD CREST

by Jessica Burkhart

TAKE THE REINS
BOOK 1

CHASING BLUE
BOOK 2

BEHIND THE BIT
BOOK 3

TRIPLE FAULT
BOOK 4

BEST ENEMIES
BOOK 5

LITTLE WHITE LIES
BOOK 6

RIVAL REVENGE
BOOK 7

HOME SWEET DRAMA
BOOK 8

CITY SECRETS
BOOK 9

Don't forget to check out the website for downloadables, quizzes, author vlogs, and more!

www.canterwoodcrest.com

FROM ALADDIN M!X   PUBLISHED BY SIMON & SCHUSTER